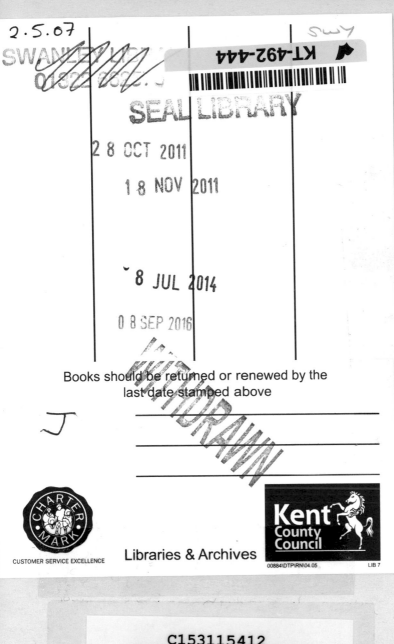

The WICKIT Chronicles

Ely Plot

THE WICKIT Chronicles

Ely Plot

by Joan Lennon

ANDERSEN PRESS

First published in Great Britain in 2007
by Andersen Press Limited
20 Vauxhall Bridge Road
London SW1V 2SA
www.andersenpress.co.uk
www.joanlennon.co.uk
www.wickitchronicles.com

Text © Joan Lennon, 2007
Illustration © David Wyatt, 2007

British Library Cataloguing in Publication Data available.
ISBN 978 184 270 595 7

Printed and bound in Great Britain
by Bookmarque Ltd., Croydon, Surrey

For William W.E. Heitler
(W.E. = Webmeister Extraordinaire)

Acknowledgements

I'd like to thank my agent Lindsey Fraser for being the best combination Rottweiler - Basset Fauve de Bretagne an author could possibly ask for. I'd also like to thank Liz Maude and Rona Selby at Andersen Press for championing the Wickit Chronicles from the start.

Contents

Chapter One - *The Day Before Autumn*   12

Chapter Two - *The Source of the Sneeze*   22

Chapter Three - *Wickit*   26

Chapter Four - *Dribbles and Pikes*   33

Chapter Five - *The Turning of the Year*   39

Chapter Six - *Complications*   45

Chapter Seven - *To Ely*   53

Chapter Eight - *Ginger Root and Cinnamon*   60

Chapter Nine - *Face the Music*   69

Chapter Ten - *Perfect's Dream*   77

Chapter Eleven - *Too Many Questions*   81

Chapter Twelve - *The Lady Chapel*   84

Chapter Thirteen - *The Royal Rooms*   93

Chapter Fourteen - *Demons and Dwale*   99

Chapter Fifteen - *Sir Robert Makes a Mess*   105

Chapter Sixteen - *Into the Night*   111

Chapter Seventeen - *Pursued*   120

Chapter Eighteen - *What the Morning Showed*   130

Chapter Nineteen - *Sanctuary*   135

Chapter Twenty - *God's Eyebrows!*   140

Brother Gilbert

Prior Benet

Brother Barnard

Abbot Michael

Brother John

Brother Paul

Wickit Monastery:

Abbot Michael - the chief monk, the father of the community

Prior Benet - second-in-command

Brother Gilbert - the Infirmarer - the monk in charge of medical care, including making medicines

Brother Barnard - the Cellarer - the monk in charge of food and provisions

Brother Paul - Wickit's handyman

Brother John

Pip

Perfect

Perfect

Pip

London:

King Arnald

Sir Giles

Sir Robert

Ely:

Bishop of Ely

Brother Mark - Precentor of Ely
Cathedral - the monk in charge
of the music

Alf - Head Choirboy

King Arnald

Sir Robert

Sir Giles

Chapter 1

The Day Before Autumn

It could just as easily have been a horrible day – grey and wet with a nasty east wind, so that climbing onto the roof was much too dangerous to even consider. But it wasn't. It was hot and clear and still, a reminder of the best of summer, tucked in right before the autumn began.

They were in the kitchen of the monastery at Wickit, listening to Brother Paul trying to talk himself into having a good look at the church roof before the weather broke. It had to be done. He knew it had to be done. But Brother Paul did not like heights.

(If you didn't know him, you might think he was too slight to have any strength in him anyway.

12

But you'd be wrong. His wiry muscles were like steel.)

'Take the boy,' Brother Barnard the Cellarer boomed, wiping his hands on a rag. 'He's big enough now to be of use to you.' Years of bending over hot ovens and open hearths had given him a brick-red face, practically the same colour as his curly russet hair. In many ways, Brother Barnard was like his kitchen – warm, friendly . . . and noisy. He wasn't a particularly large man, but he had a *very* large voice. You could hear him singing, tunelessly, above the clattering of pots, and above everyone else in a service. He made Prior Benet close his eyes and wince several times a day.

Pip looked up from the skillet he was scouring. He'd never be *that* big (which was why the monks had called him Pip in the first place), but he *had* been growing in the last half year or so. And climbing around on the roof sounded pretty good.

'Take the boy and save me having to patch up the pieces of you if you decide to fall off the ladder again,' urged Brother Gilbert. He was the Infirmarer, and one of Pip's favourites among the Brothers. He had a wide, kind, ugly face like a frog's and big blunt hands and a voice you knew you could trust, and there wasn't much he didn't know about both the diseases and the cures the Fenland had on offer. Fever and rot, hacking cough and rheumy eye, joint ache and running bowels – Brother Gilbert waged holy war against them all.

'I'll have to go anyway,' protested Brother Paul, screwing up his weathered face. 'He won't know what he's looking at!'

'Fair enough, fair enough – just let him do the scrambling, for all our sakes,' said Brother Gilbert. 'Try to stay out of my Infirmary!'

Which was how it happened that Pip was on the roof of the church of Wickit that fine day, instead of doing any of a thousand other jobs about the place. Everything that came afterwards, led on from this . . .

The monastery at Wickit had been there for as long as anyone could remember. It wasn't very big – like everybody in the vast Fens, the monks built on an island, and even in the driest year there wasn't a lot of land for it to be big *on*. Wickit was an irregular blob of ground surrounded by rushes and reeds and mud – and water.

But this wasn't *simple* water, like in a river or

in a lake. Fen water was sly, secretive, some would even say malicious. It liked to disguise itself. A bit that looked innocently open and calm could turn out to be a sucking bog. A stretch of bright green grass might be only a skin over sudden dark depths. What appeared to be a straight clear channel through the reeds could easily begin to bend as soon as you were in it, and then split into many channels, narrower and narrower until the rushes leaned in tight from all around and there was no turning back. There were floating islands, and strange noises in the marshland too, like the muddy sucking of some huge animal's feet creeping closer. And then there were the lights – Will-o'-the-Wisps, Will of the Wykes, the Lantern Man's wavering flame – that lured the unwary and the desperate into the reed maze and then swallowed them up. Different parts of the Fenland gave the phenomenon different names – but *everybody* feared it.

You *needed* a church in a place like that.

One grateful traveller went so far as to leave money to the monks in his will – enough to replace the old wooden church with a sturdy stone one. The money ran out before the building could be finished off with a spire, however, so there was only a stumpy tower on its roof.

The church was new when Pip came to Wickit. He had been little more than a baby, when his mother, crazy with the Fen fever, somehow managed to get to the monastery island with him, before dropping down in the mud and dying. In spite of all his medical skills, Brother Gilbert had had his work cut out, keeping this small scrap of humanity alive, but he managed. The church had a settled look now, and the stone was beginning to weather a little. Luckily, Brother Paul could keep *anything* in repair, whether it was made of wood, metal, reed or stone. He just preferred having his feet on the ground when he did it.

'Stone doesn't grow on trees, you know,' he grumbled to Pip as they poked and tapped and tested to see which of the roof tiles were secure and which had shifted. 'Look at the state of that! Where am I supposed to get replacements? At least with the old church you had all the roofing material you could ask for, right on the doorstep.' He gestured at the reed beds, stretching away into the hazy distance – then remembered how high up he was, and clutched at the ladder again.

They worked along steadily. Pip was *not* afraid of heights, and swarmed over the stone tiles like a cat, which caused Brother Paul to change colour quite a lot. At length, they reached the west end, and Brother Paul began to gather up his hammers and tuck them into his belt.

'Well, that's us done,' he said. 'This side anyway. Come on down now.'

'But what about the tower?' Pip objected. 'We haven't checked that.' Then, 'What's it like, Brother? Can you see all the way to Ely from up there? Can you see the sea?'

Brother Paul didn't look at him. He mumbled something.

'Sorry, Brother?' said Pip.

Another mumble, which sounded surprisingly like 'I don't know.'

Pip stared.

'You don't *know*?!' he squeaked. 'You mean, you've never been up into the tower? Never checked it? In all these years?'

This was astonishing. Brother Paul was always so workmanlike. 'Catch a problem before it *is* a problem, and you'll never have to fix it!' he liked to say.

'Yes, well?!' Brother Paul snapped. 'It hasn't leaked, has it? Best lead they used for the floor of that tower, cambered just right, drainage runnels . . . ' But bluster didn't come naturally to him. He stopped.

'I was too scared,' he admitted.

Pip reached over and patted him on the shoulder. 'Don't worry,' he said, trying not to sound smug. 'I'll go and have a look for you.'

Pip was feeling pleasantly superior, which was not a usual emotion for him. It wasn't that he didn't like Brother Paul – he did! – it was just that it didn't happen very often, him being better at something than somebody else. Part of him felt guilty, but most of him was enjoying it too much to care.

He started getting cocky.

He grabbed one of the hammers, launched himself up the roof at a carefree scamper and reached one-handed for the low stone wall of the tower.

At the last second Pip's foot slipped and he hung by his fingers – it was raw luck he managed to find a grip at all . . . In his mind, he immediately heard Prior Benet nagging, 'Pride goeth before the fall!' and he gulped. Heart pounding sickeningly, he dragged himself over the lip and collapsed onto the floor of the tower.

God's Eyebrows! he thought. *If Brother Paul saw that he probably fainted!*

Pip stuck his head over the parapet, and was relieved to see the monk still fiddling with his hammers.

And then he heard Prior Benet's voice *again*, in reality this time.

'Brother! Can you see that wretched boy from up there? He has work to do for me.'

Pip couldn't see the Prior and obviously the Prior couldn't see him – he must be standing close to the ladder, so the edge of the roof hid them from each other.

Oh no! Pip thought in dismay. *Not now!*

He caught Brother Paul's eye, and looked pleadingly at him.

'Please don't tell!' he whispered.

Brother Paul clucked disapprovingly.

Please?! Pip said soundlessly.

'Brother! Can you *see* him?!' Prior Benet was not a patient man.

Brother Paul sighed. Then he put one hand in front of his eyes (while tightening his grip on the ladder with the other).

'I *did* see him, not long ago,' he called down in a solemn voice. 'But I can't see him now.'

Pip smothered a giggle with his fist. He could hear Prior Benet's angry snort. He still couldn't see him, but it wasn't exactly hard to picture what the monk would be looking like – an angry Prior Benet was pretty much all Pip ever *did* see, a tall, bony, beaky man, like a bad-tempered heron.

'But *I'll* be glad to come and help you,' Brother Paul continued, and he started to climb carefully down. 'Then I will return to the repairs of this roof.' Just before his head disappeared below the level of the eaves, he looked up at Pip, and winked.

Pip lay back on the sun-warmed lead and crowed inside his head. He'd thought he knew every place at Wickit where it was possible to be out of sight, but *this* . . .! This was a little kingdom in the sky that *nobody* (except Brother Paul) knew about. Pip squinted happily into the blue, humming softly, letting the sounds of the monastery drift up to him as if from far, far away. Soon the warm sun made him feel sleepy and he fell into a wonderful daydream in which Prior Benet was offering him sugared almonds and saying, 'I couldn't have been more *delighted*, Your Grace, when I heard the King had made you Archbishop of all England . . .'

. . . when he heard someone sneeze. Pip stopped breathing. The sound had come from right behind him, from the corner of the tower.

He was not alone.

The Source of the Sneeze

Pip rolled over and onto his knees in one swift movement.

'Who's there . . . ' he whispered, then the words died away in his mouth. He was staring into the corner of the tower where someone had carved a beautifully life-like pattern of leaves and flowers and fruit onto the stone of the wall. And there, from amongst the leaves, staring back at him, was . . .

. . . a gargoyle. A small gargoyle, made of stone, in the shape of a dragon, with claws and wings and a long tail and big eyes. The workmanship was so good that Pip could almost swear he saw the dragon's sides moving in and out as it breathed. He could almost swear he saw those big eyes *blink*.

Don't be stupid! he told himself.

And then it sneezed again.

'Tickly nose,' it said, as if that explained everything.

Something in Pip's brain registered the fact that the dragon's voice sounded . . . female.

'Who *are* you?!' he gasped.

The little gargoyle drew herself up to her full height – about 15 centimetres. 'My name is Perfect,' she said. 'Perfect Parting Gift.'

'Sorry?' said Pip.

'That's what my maker called me. That's his mark, there.' She pointed at a 'V' carved amongst the stone leaves on the wall. 'I remember the day he finished – he smiled at me and stroked my head and gave me my name. "You're Perfect," he said. "My Perfect Parting Gift." And then . . . I never saw him again.'

A tear trickled down her snout and she licked it away with a long tongue.

'I've just got one name,' said Pip humbly. 'The Brothers took me in when I was a baby and they called me Pip, because I was as small as a pip, you see.' His voice got lower. 'I don't remember my parents at all.'

The gargoyle looked puzzled.

'Parents?' she said. 'What's that? Is it like your maker?'

'Er . . . I guess. Yes. Pretty much.' Pip rubbed his nose. 'They died. That was a bad year for Fen fever, Brother Gilbert told me.'

There was a sad little pause between the two, but curiosity was stronger.

'*I've* been with the Brothers – but what have *you* been doing all these years?' asked Pip.

'Well,' said the dragon, 'I've been staring, mostly. Have you noticed what a fabulous view you get from up here? And then, sometimes, I catch flies. And I sleep. But no, really, it's been pretty much all staring.'

Pip was appalled. 'Staring?! For *years*?!?'

Perfect looked surprised. 'I'm a gargoyle,' she said. 'It's what we do.'

Pip thought about this for a moment. 'But – how do you *know* about what gargoyles do?' he asked. 'Did you ever meet one? Another one, I mean?'

The dragon shrugged a small stony shoulder. 'I don't know. I just *do*. Does it matter?'

Pip suddenly grinned. 'No,' he said. 'It doesn't matter at all!'

Perfect grinned back. 'Come to think of it, though,' she added shyly, 'it has been a bit lonely—'

She was interrupted by a clumping noise from down on the ground.

'It's Brother Paul,' said Pip anxiously. 'He's coming back for me. We were working on the roof before – I'll have to go. I don't think . . .'

There was a pause as the climbing sounds came closer. The dragon and the boy looked at each other, wide-eyed.

'Don't go!'

'Come with me!' Pip and Perfect said both at once.

'But I'm scared!' whispered Perfect.

'Don't worry – I'll keep you safe!' Pip whispered back. 'Here, hide inside my hood.'

'Coast is clear, boy!' It was Brother Paul, calling from the top of the ladder. 'Come down now. Hurry – it's the Abbot asking for you now!'

'Coming, Brother.' Pip scooped Perfect up – she was surprisingly light, and warm to the touch – and let her pore over his shoulder and down into his hood. 'Coming!'

Chapter 3

Wickit

Since old Brother Francis died peacefully in his sleep a few years earlier, the monastery was down to half a dozen Brothers, so some of the jobs had to be doubled up.

Abbot Michael had taken charge of Pip's schooling, and Pip was very grateful – it might have been Prior Benet! Lessons with the Abbot weren't bad at all. Teacher and pupil liked each other. (Abbot Michael was, of course, duty-bound to love the members of his flock equally, but that was not reason to expect him to *like* them all the same!) And as Pip grew older, they both came to enjoy their times together more and more.

Abbot Michael was not a fenman. His soft

Welsh voice gave him away within a few words. Once, at the end of a lesson, Pip dared to ask how he'd come to be so far away from home.

'I was restless as a lad,' Abbot Michael said quietly. 'I wanted to see the world. And somehow, here' – he put his gnarled hand to his heart – 'I always believed I could go back. I was young and very foolish. And of course I never *did* get back again.'

'Did you miss it, Father? Where you grew up, I mean.'

'I missed the hills. The truth is, it was like a broken bone in me at first, and every time I raised my eyes it was like the raw ends grating not to see them all about. But bones set in time, and some pain you just get used to. Familiar. And, well, it's all God's sky, isn't it?'

He turned to Pip and smiled, friendly but firm as well, to let him know not to ask any more.

'And "the sky of God" in Latin is . . . ?'

Latin was all right, but it was the singing lessons that Pip and the Abbot really loved. Today, though, Abbot Michael could tell he hadn't the boy's full attention.

'Where's your voice, Pip? I can barely hear you, and we're in the same room!'

'Sorry, Father.'

'Remember what I taught you: *Aim* your notes, boy! Aim them like arrows and you're the bow. Look' – and he drew Pip to the window and pointed out – 'See Prior Benet there?'

Pip looked. Way over the other side of the island, he saw Sly the fisherman, squatting sullenly in his punt with his head down. And looming over him, bent forward and finger wagging, telling him off about something, was Prior Benet.

'I see him,' said Pip. He was paying attention now!

'Aim, my son. Aim.' Abbot Michael's voice was mild and gave nothing away.

'Yes, Father.'

Pip took a deep breath, found the note in his head, focused on Prior Benet's bony backside – and let it fly.

The Prior's jump was deeply satisfying (though he did not do a complete belly-flop into the water as Pip might have wished). He did land in the soft muck at the water's edge, however. After he'd pulled his foot out of the mud, and then retrieved his shoe, he swung round angrily . . . and stared. There was no one near. Only the Abbot, looking down at him from his window, right the

28

other side of the island. The Abbot raised a hand in blessing, and Prior Benet crossed himself, bewildered, while Fisher Sly hid a grin in his hands.

Pip's day just kept getting better. At Vespers, he sang a high, clear descant to the Benedictus so beautifully that everyone except Prior Benet smiled at their prayers. And all through the service he could feel Perfect curled up in his hood, warm against his back and humming quietly along to the music.

Then, just before bedtime, Brother Paul came to the kitchen.

'You were a good help today, boy,' he said. 'On the roof. Thank you.'

Pip blushed – he wasn't used to being treated in such a grown-up way.

'I . . . I was glad to, Brother,' he said. Then, as the monk turned to go, he added, 'Er . . . could I ask you a question?'

Brother Paul looked round enquiringly.

'I was wondering . . . Who was "V", Brother?'

Brother Paul looked blank.

'I saw his mark, up in the tower. I thought you'd know who he was,' Pip went on. 'Who was it worked on the tower, when the church was built?'

Brother Paul scratched the shaved patch on

his head. (His hair always grew back faster than anybody else's, and in between shaving times, his tonsure was mostly itchy stubble.) Then it came to him. 'V,' he said. 'That would be the foreign chap. Vincenzi, he was called. What a master! Knew stone, that man did, like a mother knows her child.' He shook his head, remembering. 'But I'll tell you some things I noticed about Vincenzi,' he went on, 'just little things, mind you, but they made me think . . . he was no stranger to monastic life.'

'What do you mean?' Pip stared. '*What* did you see?'

Brother Paul looked uncomfortable. It was a Rule of the Order not to gossip – indeed it was a Rule not to speak at all unless it was necessary – but Brother Paul was an incurably chatty soul, and it *was* a good story. Besides, it was just to the boy, so it didn't *really* count . . . He leaned closer.

'Well . . . *twice* I saw him make as if to tuck a habit up through his belt before climbing a ladder, and then look impatient with himself. But more than that, it was the way *he always knew what time it was*. He'd look up, just before the bell would ring for every service – never left a job unfinished – like he'd grown so used to how much time he'd have between one service and the next that he'd set his work to fit the space, if you follow me. He never missed Matins either, though no one *expects* laymen to attend church at 3:00 in the morning . . .'

'So you think he used to be a monk? He used to be a monk and then . . . he *quit*?!' Pip couldn't imagine anyone he knew ever leaving the Order. In his experience, it just didn't *happen*!

Brother Paul tapped the side of his nose and said nothing.

'And then what happened?' asked Pip.

'Nothing happened. The money for the church ran out, so the work stopped and he left. I remember him saying, at the end, "I am going home now, in the time I have left."'

'What did he mean?'

Brother Paul shook his head. 'I think he wasn't a well man, lad. I think he knew he hadn't long to live. God rest him.'

Only Pip heard the little whimper from inside his hood.

'Well, goodnight, boy.' And Brother Paul headed off to the monks' dormitory.

Pip slept in the kitchen by himself, unless the monastery had guests. Now he banked the fire, and laid his straw pallet out near the warmth.

'Perfect?' he whispered. 'Are you all right?'

He felt her claws snag in the rough wool of his tunic as she climbed up to his shoulder and then down his sleeve. She sat on his forearm like a little bird of prey and looked at him, her big eyes glittering in the firelight.

'Are you all right?' he asked again, carefully stroking the rough top of her head with his finger. For a moment she held herself rigid . . . then, without becoming any less stony, Pip felt her relax.

'Yes, Pip,' said Perfect. 'I'm all right. Now.'

Chapter 4

Dribbles and Pikes

It was one of Pip's jobs to scrape the dribbles and globs of wax off the candlesticks, off the floor, off the wall . . . Making candles was a kitchen job, and Wickit's candles were made of whatever Brother Barnard could get his hands on – leftovers of lard, pig fat, tallow. During services, they smoked and spat and stank and generally made a mess, and Pip hated them. He'd made himself a number of different-sized scrapers from bits of wood, but a lot of the work could only be done by fingernail. It made his hands smell of rancid fat and he was forever picking bits of yuck out from under his nails.

The first time Perfect joined him inside the

church, he was down on his knees, scraping away at a patch of spilled wax on the rough stone of the floor. He was only succeeding in spreading the greasy mess about, and he was getting more fed up by the minute. The dragon watched him for a while, perched at her ease on the front edge of the pulpit. Finally she commented, 'You missed a bit.'

Pip growled.

'You're not doing a very good job of that at all, really,' she added.

'And *you* could do better?!' Pip snapped.

'Oh, yes. If you'd like to step aside?'

Pip dragged himself up off his knees with a poor grace.

'Look, I really don't have time to waste . . .' he began, but Perfect was already on the job.

She lay on her tummy, her chin on the cold floor, and flamed, gently. As soon as the wax had softened she was up and licking, her sandpaper tongue lapping faster than a cat's at a forbidden cream bowl.

'Tasty!' she chirped, and moved on to the next flagstone.

Pip stared.

Her flame control really was very impressive. For example, she was able to soften wax on the walls without scorching the paintwork, and the merest flicker of flame left every crevice and curly bit of the candlesticks ready for licking. *And* she managed to stay clean herself, which Pip found almost as amazing as her ability to turn this most tedious task into a picnic. Perfect never smelled of anything except warm stone, a scent Pip had always liked anyway.

A lot of his jobs were too heavy or too public for Perfect to help with, but even when she had to stay out of sight she was still *company*. Pip hadn't really realised before just how lonely he'd been, just how much he needed a friend.

At night, she slept on his straw pallet by the kitchen fire, tucked into his blanket. During the day, she hid in his hood when need be, or in his tunic, or simply attached herself high up on a wall or roof beam and became unnoticeable. When the Brothers sent him on errands to their scattered parishioners, or to fish, or collect plants for Brother Gilbert's pharmacy (Perfect had an excellent nose for green things), she liked to sit on the prow of the monastery punt like a pint-sized figurehead. The two felt free on the water, away from prying eyes and safe. Though there were some things that *weren't* a good idea . . .

'You don't want to do that,' Pip said, pointing at her tail hanging down into the water.

'Why not?' said Perfect. 'It feels nice. I want to do it!'

'Not in this pond,' said Pip. 'This is Patrick Jerome's pond, and he doesn't like trespassers.'

Perfect looked surprised. 'I didn't know a fisherman could own a pond!' she said.

Pip shook his head. 'Patrick Jerome's not a fisherman,' he said. 'Watch.' And he took a bit of bread from his lunch and threw it out onto the surface of the water.

There was a moment's pause – and then, so suddenly it made Perfect leap into the air with a squeal, the bread was engulfed by a set of jaws that looked to her to be as big as the boat itself. There was a passing glimpse of a long, pointed snout and mad, mean eyes, before the huge fish disappeared again, leaving only a disturbing ripple behind as evidence.

'Patrick Jerome's a pike,' said Pip smugly. 'Must weigh as much as me, almost.'

It isn't possible for a gargoyle to go pale, but Perfect's eyes did get incredibly big, and she gulped audibly.

'Takes birds, too,' Pip continued. 'Comes up

underneath, grabs them by the feet, and drags them under.' He made a horrible glooping noise, and grinned.

Perfect kept her tail tightly curled round her feet after that. In fact it was ages before he could convince her it was safe to go back in the water, but fish like Patrick Jerome are very territorial, and only like particular types of hunting-ground.

Perfect *loved* to swim, which was surprising, of course, since things made of stone generally don't. At first Pip fretted about her the whole time she was out of his sight – what if she got tangled in some water lily roots? What if a heron mistook her for a fish and speared her? What if pike *weren't* as territorial as he thought they were? And what if somebody saw her? But he needn't have worried. She was as at home in the water as an eel, and just as agile.

When he asked her, 'How is it you can swim, and fly? You're a *gargoyle* – you're made of stone!' she just looked at him.

'I'm a *dragon* gargoyle-made-of-stone,' she said. 'How could I not be able to swim and fly?!'

And that had been that. (Though, to be honest, she couldn't really fly *far*, and tended to get quite out of breath doing it.)

Although it was never discussed openly between them, they both knew that Perfect must be kept a secret. Pip had no exact idea what would happen if someone found out that part of Wickit Church could talk, and was currently spending time in the boy's hood – but he was sure it would be nothing good. The punishments for witchcraft or sorcery or having to do with suspected demons were too awful to think about.

There were some close calls, but Pip was always able to say, 'That? Oh, I think it was an owl' or 'Yes, the rats *are* big this year' or even 'I didn't see anything. What did you think you saw?' To which no one was likely to answer, 'I think I saw a gargoyle that talks.'

Chapter 5

The Turning of the Year

As the year slid down into winter, Pip grew some more, and continued to get on Prior Benet's nerves on a regular basis. Perfect always talked about the Prior as 'the Bad Brother' – she was not good at remembering names, but she was very clear on who was Pip's friend, and who wasn't. One of the triumphs of the season for her was the time she managed to dislodge a great clump of snow off the church roof, so that it landed on Prior Benet's bare head as he strode by. She didn't stop giggling for days.

Abbot Michael worried everyone by catching a bad cold that threatened to become something worse. But Brother Gilbert doctored him with mustard poultices and drafts of lungwort and thyme and liquorice; Brother Barnard made him possets and junkets and broth in the kitchen; Pip built the fire up in his room day and night; everybody prayed hard – and he got better.

Brother Paul kept the buildings weather-tight. Pip learned Latin, and sang, and loved every minute of his time with Perfect.

And, throughout it all, the pattern of life at Wickit carried on, unchanging against the backdrop of change, with eel pie appearing on the menu with monotonous regularity.

Meanwhile, far away in the great world outside the Fens, the year moved towards Christmas in London too.

As the crow flies, it was no more than a daytrip from the marshes to the great city. As the human trudges, the way was far harder, longer, indirect, and dangerous. The roads were appallingly bad and difficult to move along, whatever the time of year, and in the winter, conditions only got worse. There were other dangers too – dispossessed men lived in the forests, outlaws with nothing left to lose. Travellers were easy prey. And if robbers didn't get you, there were plenty of packs of wolves. Or you might simply lose yourself in the great woods and die of exposure without any other interference at all.

Not that the city itself was safe. From cutpurses to cutthroats, London teemed with human predators. Without sanitation, disease was everywhere. The poor died daily of fluxes, fevers and agues, unnoticed in corners and alleyways. More fuss was made when the rich fell ill, but it made little difference in the end. It was a fragile thing, life, as easily snuffed out as a candle.

And what of the King? Men at arms always surrounded him. He had an army to defend him against enemies from abroad. No one could guard him from disease, of course, but he was at least always well fed and warm, and didn't have to share a bed with three other people and their fleas. But there were threats to a king's life that had nothing to do with the Black Death.

Arnald was not quite fourteen when his father died suddenly. He'd never known his mother, who died when he was born. There was an immediate scramble of people who were very keen indeed to take their places for him, but their motives didn't have much to do with pity for the royal orphan. Power was where the King was, and the closer you could get to the King, the more of it could be yours.

The coronation was rushed through on the heels of the old king's funeral, but the plotting didn't stop there. In the corridors of the King's great house, noblemen gathered to whisper and connive. And it wasn't just influence they had on their minds.

It was curious how people managed to believe with absolute sincerity that the King's authority came direct from God AND that the nobles had the right to remove a monarch they didn't like. Everyone *said*, 'Long Live the King' – but in Arnald's case, the odds weren't good. Too many people were of the opinion that his cousin Frederick would be a more manipulable monarch. Or his uncle, currently in exile in France. And some of these people were willing to back their opinions with action . . .

One cold afternoon, two lords, meeting in a corridor,

eyed each other suspiciously.

'Sir Robert?'

'Sir Giles?'

'I go to attend the King.'

'I also.'

'After you.'

'No, after *you*.'

'Ah, well, we'll go together then.'

So the two noblemen continued, side by side. But, *Together*? they each thought. *Not on your life!*

And later the same day, there was another meeting – in a corner of the city's great cathedral, between a clergyman of high standing and one of these fine gentlemen. But in spite of the setting, it was not the spiritual condition of either of them that they were discussing.

'The Bishop of London is nothing but a crawler, Your Grace,' the nobleman murmured. 'But the King is only a boy, and easily impressed by showmanship and flattery.'

'Well? What do you suggest I do about it?' the clergyman snapped. 'The Bishop of London has his ear entirely now, after all his feasting and mummers and music.'

'Christmas is his, Your Grace, no doubt. But children have short memories. Invite the King to Ely for Easter . . . impress him with *your* hospitality . . . see if you can't win him to you after the long rigours of Lent.'

'And if I can't persuade him even then?'

The nobleman's smile showed faintly in the dim light, like a predator waiting in the shadows.

'A king who cannot be persuaded, Your Grace, can always be removed . . .'

Complications

Every year, two monks from Wickit made the trip to Ely, to resupply after the long winter, and to take part in the services at the great Cathedral. But *this* year there was one complication after another. Holy Week came early and the weather was still very uncertain. At first, it was decided that Prior Benet and Brother John were to go, and a local man was asked to ferry them. But it had been such a hard winter that no family felt they could spare anyone that long. Prior Benet was all set to *demand* their obedience, but Abbot Michael insisted the people's help must be freely given. And then Brother John slipped on a patch of icy mud and broke his wrist. So, Brother *Gilbert* was to take his place, which solved the ferrying problem, since *he* was perfectly at home in a punt and didn't need anyone extra to help. It also meant he could do his own shopping for the Infirmary – there were some things he badly needed to restock. He spent days muttering about cinnamon and myrrh, St. John's wort and vervain, greater celandine and shepherd's purse – but in the end . . .

'Brother Gilbert has told me he feels he really cannot leave the Infirmary just now,' said Abbot Michael. 'It's been a long winter, and the fever's spreading again.'

Pip felt his stomach tighten. It always did when the Fen fever was mentioned. When he went round with Brother Gilbert to the huts of the fishermen and the reed-cutters and the peat-diggers, he found himself seeing his mother or his father in every suffering face. Strange, really, that he could miss his parents so much, when he'd no memory of them at all.

Still, Brother Gilbert maintained that, having survived the illness as a baby, he was unlikely to get it again. 'Some things God only asks of us the once,' he said.

Right now, Pip wasn't sure what he was doing here. The summons had come just after breakfast, and he'd assumed he was in for some extra Latin. Perfect, who only really enjoyed singing lessons, had abandoned him to spend time on the roof. But when Pip arrived at the Abbot's room, Prior Benet and Brother John were there as well.

'So Brother Gilbert will not be going to Ely after all,' continued Abbot Michael.

'But he *must*!' exclaimed Prior Benet. 'I cannot go *alone*, Father!' He sounded thoroughly shocked. 'Brothers must *always* travel in twos when they go into the world, to keep watch on each other's conduct, to keep each other safe from Satan and sin – the Rule is extremely clear on that.'

Pip tried to imagine either Prior Benet, or Brother Gilbert, for that matter, giving in to any of the temptations of the world, but he just couldn't. There were no sins the Prior would find even remotely attractive, and Brother Gilbert probably wouldn't notice Satan until he'd come up and bitten him on the nose. *Then* he'd probably just stare at the Arch-demon and ask him about the state of his bowels.

Abbot Michael gave a tiny sigh. 'I know the Rule, my son,' he said. 'Which is why I have decided that Brother John will come with you, as originally planned. It's only his arm that has been injured, after all – his eyes are as sharp as ever,' he concluded. The Abbot did not add that this was not, in fact, saying much.

Brother John was . . . unique. For one thing, it was almost impossible to tell how old he was. The hair round his tonsure was a sort of non-colour that might have been white or just a very pale blond, and his face was as wide-eyed and unwrinkled as a child's. It was also true that he *could not* see the bad side of anyone or anything. Depending on your own nature, this made him either the most calming person imaginable to be around, or the most irritating.

Brother John smiled his open, innocent smile. 'A trip to Ely?!' he said. 'Thank you, Father!'

'You're welcome,' said Abbot Michael.

'Then we will have to *make* a fenman take us,' interrupted Prior Benet with a quite unseemly vehemence. '*I* can't punt!'

48

Abbot Michael nodded his head solemnly. 'It *is* much trickier than it looks,' he murmured.

'I meant,' the Prior grated through clenched teeth, 'I meant, I am the *Prior*. It would not be *appropriate* for me to arrive at Ely wielding a pole . . .'

'Is that what they call it?' said Brother John, bemused. '"Wielding?" I've never heard it called that before—'

'*Whatever it's called!*'

'I'm sure *I* could pick it up though, this wielding, you know, with a little instruction from young Pip here, even with this foolish injury!' he said brightly, waving his good arm about in what he probably thought was a muscly and capable way.

'I will keep your offer in mind for the future, my son,' said Abbot Michael gravely. '*This* time, however, I have decided that Pip himself will be going to Ely with you and so no other arrangement for your transportation needs to be made. I . . .'

Pip didn't hear any more. The Abbot was still speaking but Pip's brain had got stuck in delight. *I'm going to Ely! I'm going to Ely!* he was singing to himself, when he was dragged back to attention by Prior Benet's voice.

'But just look at him!' he was exclaiming. 'He cannot enter Ely Cathedral in pig-muck and rags and mud and, and . . . he is disgraceful!!'

There was a pause in which the Prior's outraged breathing could be distinctly heard.

Then Abbot Michael spoke, quietly, sweetly, but the metal underneath was suddenly clear to everyone in the room.

'Disgraceful . . . I cannot think you really mean the child is outside God's grace – full of grace-less-ness. I'm sure, my son, you do not mean that. *But* you do have a point . . .'

Pip's heart sank like a rock in muck.

'. . . so new clothes will need to be bought. A complete set. If he is to sing with a real choir, he must be presentable.' The Abbot tutted, ignoring Pip's dumbfounded expression. 'You are absolutely right. He has outgrown his hose and tunic completely, and just look – that cloak will be lace before we know where we are!'

'But Father – the expense!' Prior Benet made one last attempt. 'We are too small a monastery to afford—'

'I have been my own Bursar long enough, my son, to *know* what Wickit can afford. You may go now, both of you, and see what Brother Gilbert and the others require from Ely. Pip, stay with me a moment longer, please.'

The two monks left, Prior Benet rigid with disapproval, Brother John twittering happily. There was a moment's silence in the room, during which Pip squirmed and Abbot Michael watched him, humming gently.

'You *are* ready, you know,' he said at last. 'It's time for you to sing with a real choir.'

Pip stared at his disreputable shoes. 'I'm grateful, Father . . . I *am* . . . Going to Ely! And new clothes! But . . . *singing*?! I'm *sure* they won't let me. I mean, I can't just stroll up to the Precentor of Ely Cathedral and say, "You don't know me, but I really think you should let me sing in your extremely famous choir!"'

Abbot Michael raised an eyebrow. 'You could if the Precentor knew *me*. Brother Mark and I both trained under Precentor Mattias – and I've told you about *him*! Everything I know I learned from Mattias – and everything I know I've taught to you. And now Brother Mark's the Cathedral Precentor at Ely and – well, it's time I sent him a little gift!'

Pip looked up in horror. 'Father, you can't . . . it's just . . . couldn't I just go and *listen*?! Couldn't I—'

But Abbot Michael was shaking his head, and Pip knew better than to argue with the expression on his face. Abbot Michael could look as mild as milk sometimes, but he had a will like a rock *and* a hard place, put together.

Pip heaved a great sigh and went to get ready.

Chapter 7

To Ely

'. . . and don't pay more than the price I told you for the saffron, and make sure the ginger isn't old stock . . .'

Pip nodded dutifully, hiding a yawn. It was the morning of Maundy Thursday, the day before Good Friday. Brother Gilbert had had him up half the night, memorising his long shopping list of medicinal spices and herbs, and now he had a full day of punting ahead of him in the cold. It was hard to believe it was practically spring – the Fen lay shivering under a blanket of icy fog, and the slant morning sun was showing no signs of being able to break through it.

Part of Pip was longing to be off, and part of him was dreading it. He'd never been properly away from home before. Then he felt Perfect shift a little inside his tunic, and Brother John came trotting over, beaming, and he realised he was taking some of home with him.

Not to mention Prior Benet . . .

'We've no more time to waste. Brother, get in the boat.' The fog swirled to get out of the way as the Prior strode up to the water's edge and glared at them all. 'Stop dawdling, boy! Make an effort!'

Pip sighed as he pushed the punt away from the shore. It was going to be a long day.

And for the first while there was nothing but the wet whiteness to look at and the slurp of the boat through the water and the crackle of the cold-stiffened reeds on either side to hear. But then something unusual happened.

Brother John started to sing. Years and years of being a monk had given him an infallible sense of the passage of time, and he knew when the next period of prayer had come. His voice was thin but true, and he began the service quietly and unselfconsciously, miles from any church. Pip could see Prior Benet stiffen disapprovingly at first, but then he joined in, muttering the words under his breath.

Pip was amazed – and began to sing as well. As the rhythm of the punting and the rhythm of the singing came together, Pip could feel all his tiredness leave him. 'I will lift up my eyes to the hills,' he sang (in Latin, of course), thinking of Abbot Michael, and Brother John replied, 'From whence cometh my help.' Pip felt light, and strong, and he pushed the boat forward through the swirling mist fearlessly, as if across an open lake in the sunshine.

He almost got away with it, too. The boat flew forward safely right up until the very last verse. 'The Lord shall preserve thy going out and thy coming in from this time forth, and even for everMORE!' he sang – and the punt slammed straight into a reed bed.

Pip stayed upright by hanging onto the punt-pole, but Prior Benet and Brother John landed in a tangled heap in the bottom of the boat.

'God's Eyebrows! – Brother, your arm! – I'm so sorry—' Pip dropped to his knees and crawled forward in concern. 'Are you hurt?!'

'Not at all, boy,' Brother John gasped. 'A bit startled – not a usual part of the service, eh? – but still sound . . .'

Both the Brothers seemed to have the breath knocked out of them but no other damage done. Unless you included damage to dignity. Even in the midst of his worry for Brother John, Pip couldn't help but notice how funny Prior Benet looked with his thin white legs waving about in the air like that.

The Prior got his breath back soon enough, of course, and all the time Pip was un-wedging the boat from the reed bed and long after they were back on course, he scolded and lectured and scowled.

The worst of the fog cleared soon after, and they broke their journey at a peat-cutter's hut. The woman treated them as honoured guests, giving them the best of the food, and she seemed pleased when Brother John made friends with the children clustered shyly round her skirts. When it was time to leave, he blessed them all and thanked her especially for her hospitality. Prior Benet said nothing, and received what was given him as his due.

The short winter afternoon wore on, and then, between one push and the next, it was there –

Ely Cathedral, rising above the reeds like a chilly mirage. Pip's mouth dropped, and cold fen water ran down into his sleeves unnoticed.

You could see why they called it 'The Ship of the Fens'. It sailed above the town, gathering the last of the light to itself. Like all the islands of the Fen, Ely rose only gently above water level, but the cathedral builders had taken its highest place as their starting point. But the 'Island of Eels' was not just a dramatic place to put a cathedral. It had been a fortress island for hundreds of years, and still was – whoever held the island was in an excellent strategic position. Its defences weren't cliffs or ditches or drawbridges or spiked barricades, but the Fens themselves, as anyone who had ever tried moving troops through marshland would know. And all round the island and along the causeways, to the distance a good archer could shoot (plus a bit more for good measure) the reeds had been cut back. This wide belt of open space made sneaking up on Ely in daylight impossible – and travelling in the Fenland at *night* was just insane.

The open water was being ruffled by a small cold wind as the Wickit punt emerged from the reeds. The day was almost over and the last slanty bits of light caught the edges of the little waves and made them glint. Then the bells began – and, strangely, it was that sound more than anything his eyes were seeing that told Pip he was about to enter another world. Wickit's little handbell called them all to prayer and food, sleeping and waking, in a voice not unlike that of a relentless frog. Ely's bells did the same job, but in tones that would not have been out of place in the foremost choir of heaven.

Pip gulped, crossed himself, and continued to pole towards the pier.

'Slow down!' barked Prior Benet. 'We don't want to arrive during Vespers!'

He needn't have worried. By the time Pip moored their punt amongst the others along the pier and they'd squidged up over the muddy foreshore, through the open gate in the town wall, and on into the narrow, noisome streets, the service was finished. In the fading light Pip could barely understand what he was seeing – buildings loomed up everywhere, and the enormous bulk of the cathedral seemed to block out the sky. The monks in charge of visitors were brisk and efficient, however. The three were taken to the refectory and fed, though Pip could not have told you what he'd eaten. Then the Brothers went off to the Black

Hostelry, where visiting monks were housed, and Pip was led away to the Guest Hall for the night.

'Meet us in the cloister after breakfast. We will go into the town at that time and conduct our business.' Prior Benet gave Pip his orders in a lordly voice. Brother John smiled, and waved.

The Guest Hall was huge, and lined with beds down each wall.

'You'll sleep here, lad,' said the monk who'd brought him. 'In the morning, just follow the crowd – you'll find your way round very soon, you'll see!'

'We'll keep an eye on him, Brother!' A group of merchants had the beds across the aisle and one of them, a man with a big loud laugh who reminded Pip a little of Brother Barnard, gave him an encouraging wink.

Pip was sure he would never be able to sleep in such a place, with strangers moving about on every side, talking, laughing, preparing for the night. But as soon as he'd wrapped himself in the blanket, and Perfect had tucked her hard little head under his chin, his eyes closed irresistibly, and sleep shut all the strangeness away.

He didn't stir till morning.

Chapter 8

Ginger Root and Cinnamon

'Here I am, Brothers!'

It was still early when Pip came running up to the Wickit monks waiting in the cloister. And he *hadn't* got lost – at least not until the last moment, when he came out of the refectory by the wrong door and ended up somewhere behind the kitchen . . .

Brother John greeted him with, 'Did you sleep well?' but Prior Benet only scowled and headed for the town. Pip was too keyed up to care, and Perfect had draped herself under his tunic so that she could peek out at this fascinating new world from below Pip's right ear without being seen. Her whispers of 'Ooooo!' and 'Look at that!' were like little echoes of the over-excited whittering inside his own head.

The market had been in full swing since sunrise. Booths were set up against any convenient wall, and each vendor was trying to out-yell his neighbours: *'Buy my shoes!' 'Best fresh fish!' 'Buns! Buns! Bread and buns!'* Shoppers picked their way carefully around piles of rubbish and puddles of nightsoil emptied by householders into the streets – though, since everyone tidied up before a King came to visit, the mess wasn't as ancient as usual. Stray pigs were finding their breakfasts in the muck and doing their best to trip up unwary humans.

'Clothes for the lad?' said Brother John cheerfully, pointing at a stall, but the Prior had other plans.

'We will acquire the monastery's *essentials* first,' he stated.

Pip could tell what he was thinking. *He's hoping there won't be enough money left for my new clothes,* he thought. *He's hoping everything else will be too expensive and use it all up.*

Barley and beer, skins and meat and cakes – even at the end of the hard winter there were goods to be sold. The bulkier things were sent to the Black Hostelry to await their return. Brother Gilbert's medicinal ingredients, however, were too precious for that. Pip's basket soon began to fill, and he kept an anxious eye on the amount of money left in Prior Benet's purse.

It wasn't easy to find someone selling the more exotic items Brother Gilbert had asked for. Eventually they were directed down a particular street, a bit quieter than the others. The stalls here were larger and more permanent looking.

'There!' said Pip, pointing to a counter piled with wooden boxes and small sacks that were giving off a dizzying muddle of scents, strong enough to cut through the midden stink of the street. He could hear Perfect sniffing up the smells and purring with pleasure.

The Prior nodded curtly and started to stride forward . . .

It was at this point they realised Brother John was no longer with them.

Pip gasped.

'Where *is* he?!' demanded Prior Benet. He glared at Pip accusingly, as if it must be *his* fault they were one monk down. 'Go and *look* for him –

no, I'd better – you get started on Brother Gilbert's requirements for the Infirmary here and *I'll* find Brother John!'

He gave Pip a shove towards the stall and made off with big angry strides back the way they had come.

Pip watched him go, and then stepped up to the booth. He took a deep, appreciative sniff at the medley of fragrances, and then addressed the owner.

'Excuse me, sir, do you have a supply of goods from Arabia and the Far East?'

For a moment, the man just looked at him appraisingly, balancing Pip's ragged clothes against the basket of bought merchandise he was carrying. Then, 'I am a dealer in foreign products, yes,' he said, rocking on his heels and sticking out his chest. 'Though what interest that might be to a little eel-kisser such as yourself, I cannot imagine.'

The man had a powerful voice. At first Pip couldn't understand what he was being so noisy about – then he noticed that passers-by were slowing down and stopping. It might be a fineable offence to physically grab hold of passing customers, but there was no law against grabbing their *attention*.

Pip was to be part of a show.

Just ignore it, he advised himself. **And don't blush!**

But it was no good – the colour was already rising up Pip's neck.

He started to recite Brother Gilbert's list. 'The Infirmarer requires—' but he got no further.

'Speak up, boy!' the vendor bellowed. 'Unless your Infirmarer wants to buy something from me he shouldn't – was that a love potion you asked me for?!'

The spectators were grinning now, and more were gathering.

Face flaming, Pip tried again. 'My Infirmarer requires,' he said in a louder voice, 'a pennyworth of saffron, a half-groat sack of bark of cinnamon and another of your best ginger root—'

The vendor gave a broad wink to the crowd.

'No doubt for the treatment of plague,' he leered. 'Though we all know what ginger's *really* good for . . . !'

Pip gritted his teeth and kept going.

'And a groat's-worth of belladonna.'

'Your Infirmarer likes to kill a lot of people, then, eh?' the man interrupted again. 'Takes a lot of skill to use dwale for much else.'

'Dwale? No – I asked for—'

'Belladonna, then, if you insist on the Latin, *my Lord.*' He made an elaborate bow. 'I will be *honoured* to indulge your Lordship with the very last of my supply – you'd be surprised what a demand there's been this last while. And will you be paying for all that in *coin-us*, my Lord, or in *eel-us-us*?'

'Coin.'

Pip wouldn't have believed he could *ever* be thankful to hear Prior Benet's voice, but he was thankful now. The monk was standing behind him, tall and gaunt and disapproving, every inch a Prior.

The merchant shrivelled.

'Very good, Brother. Thank you, Brother. I'll just pack these . . .'

Pip handed over the basket and the man began to stow the medicines with elaborate care, wrapping great handfuls of straw round each purchase. The retrieved Brother John stood to one side, looking subdued.

The man named a price. It was not far off every penny they had left, and Prior Benet was just beginning to nod, when Pip spoke up.

'I can't *imagine* why you think the good Prior would not know the value of your wares,' he said loudly. Two could play at *that* game!

The man shot him a truly venomous look, but gave in.

'Of course I was only quoting the cost to *myself*,' he snarled. 'For the good and glory of the Church I would be asking . . . ' and he named a price almost exactly the same as Brother Gilbert's estimate – one that left them with an ample amount over for Pip's new clothes.

Pip walked demurely over to Brother John, who gave him a seraphic smile.

'Where'd you *go!?*' whispered Pip.

Brother John blushed. 'I was watching a juggler,' he whispered back. 'I never even realised I was lost until Brother Benet found me again! It was very kind of him.'

Pip looked over at the 'very kind' Prior, and had to hide a grin. It was hard to choose which had the sourer expression on his face as the money changed hands – the merchant or the monk.

'And now,' chirped Brother John, *'the clothes stalls!'*

Good Friday might be the day the churches lost all their finery, but it was also the day Pip became the proud owner of his. At least, the set of clothes they bought for him felt like finery, though in truth they were very ordinary stuff. *But they were new!* Pip had never had *anything* before that wasn't handed down, re-jigged, or cobbled together from somebody else's cast-offs.

He clutched the bundle of hose, shirt, tunic, hood and shoes, wrapped up in his new cloak, close to his chest with one arm, and carried the heavy basket of Wickit supplies with the other. He was watching the ground closely, taking especial care not to slip or stumble – so *much care* that Prior Benet had to grab him roughly to get him stopped.

'Fool!' he hissed, and then bowed.

Pip was so surprised he looked up, straight at a collection of superior clergy, the nobles of the royal court – and the King of England. Pip quickly crouched into a bow as the cortege sauntered by on its way to the Bishop's luxurious quarters. His brain whirred with what he had just seen.

Though King Arnald was only a few years older than Pip, he was quite a lot bigger and taller. He was wearing brightly coloured fine-woven wool, and fur, and a velvet hat. Pip couldn't believe it. *He'd just been five feet away from the King!* The King of England. God's Anointed. The Supreme—

'Not much to look at, is he?' whispered Perfect, though it seemed more like a shout to Pip. 'Spotty. Weak chin. Looks like a bit of a sulker. And whoever told him those colours suited him was no friend!'

Pip stopped breathing. He knew roughly what the punishments for treason were. He just didn't want to find out the details – first hand.

But, amazingly, their luck held. No one seemed to have heard the little voice being rude about the anointed King of All England, and Pip, his knees quivering, was able to carry on to the refectory without being arrested and dragged away in chains.

Chapter 9

Face the Music

It was after the midday meal. Prior Benet and Brother John were walking in the cloister, and Pip in his new clothes was tagging along behind them. He wasn't paying attention to anything much in particular except a bit of fish bone caught between his teeth, when suddenly one of the Ely monks pounced on him.

'There you are!' the man boomed cheerfully.

Pip bit his tongue in surprise.

'I spoke with Brother Simon earlier, Pip,' Brother John explained. 'About you and the choir, you know.'

'That's right! And I've caught up with you just in time – the Precentor will be taking the boys through for their practice right about . . . now!'

Pip stuttered, 'O-oh . . . e-er . . .' but the monk just beamed at him and, taking a good grip on the boy's sleeve, he led him away at a brisk pace.

'The boys gather outside the school, then they form up and process across to the cathedral, doing their level best to look angelic – but *we* know better, don't we!' The monk laughed heartily at his own joke. 'And there they are!'

A crowd of boys turned at the sound of his voice, and *stared* at them. Pip would have turned tail and run away, but the monk still had a firm hold on his sleeve.

'Don't be shy!' he boomed. Then he raised his voice even more. 'I've brought you a lost lamb, Brother Mark. He was wandering in the cloister with a couple of the brothers from Wickit.'

The Precentor was such a little man that he'd been completely hidden by the crowd of boys, but he pushed through them now.

'Wickit?' he said, wrinkling up his face. 'Wickit? But that's where – did Brother Michael send you? I mean, Abbot Michael, of course.'

Pip could feel himself going red.

'Yes, Brother,' he muttered. There was a rustle amongst the boys that he didn't understand.

'Splendid!' The Precentor practically sang the word. '*Abbot* Michael sent you, so you must be very, very good, eh?'

Pip was appalled.

'Oh no, Brother. Abbot Michael *never* said so.'

'And what did he say, hm? Did he ever say, um, "You'll do?"'

It felt like a test. All the boys were watching him. None of them blinked.

Pip didn't know what to say. He nodded reluctantly. 'Well, yes, Brother, he did say that.'

There was, if that were possible, an *intensifying* of attention from the choir. One boy in particular, a big lad with bad skin, was looking at him now with an inexplicable, beady-eyed loathing.

What have I done? Pip wondered to himself in panic, but the Precentor was pointing at him now and addressing the other boys.

'Who have I told you is the greatest Precentor this cathedral has ever known?'

'BROTHER MATTIAS,' they all chanted the answer.

'And what were Brother Mattias' highest words of praise?'

'YOU'LL DO,' came the chant.

71

Stop! thought Pip. *What are you doing to me?!*

But Brother Mark really seemed to have no idea of the pit he was digging for Pip. He didn't stop.

'And now Brother Mattias' best pupil is sending us his pupil – *well!* I'd say we're in for something *special!*' And the little man beamed at Pip, completely unaware of the effect of his words on him and the resident pack, now fully primed to rip the stranger's throat out at the first opportunity.

Before he could add anything to make it even worse, however, the Precentor was called aside by a novice who bustled up and whispered a message into his ear.

The Precentor looked mildly annoyed.

'All right,' he said, 'I'll see to it.' And then in a louder voice, 'Carry on, boys. Wait for me in the Porch. I won't be a minute.'

The choir formed up in twos and set off at a sedate pace, ignoring Pip, who trailed along behind.

As they crossed the open space by the cathedral in which he was about to sing, he knew he should be feeling inspired and uplifted – but he didn't. He felt awful. Everything here was too *big*. He stared up at the height of the great church and couldn't quite believe that anything could reach so far into the sky and not collapse under the weight of its own pride. Parts of the building *had* fallen down. The front of the cathedral was lopsided now, since the enormous left-hand tower had caved in. And the Octagon – that astonishing, revolutionary, eight-sided construction – two hundred tons of timber, glass and lead supported on eight massive stone pillars – was the replacement for a much older tower that collapsed. Pip couldn't imagine what that must have been like, all the weight of stone suddenly crashing down. Had they had any warning? A crack in a wall? An ominous creaking? Had it just *happened?!* Or—

Still goggling upward, Pip walked straight into the back of the boy in front of him. The procession had stopped respectfully to let a number of monks pass by.

'Watch out, stupid,' the boy snarled back at him without turning his head.

'Sorry,' Pip muttered, but the boy didn't answer.

He made it to the great front Porch of the cathedral without any more trouble, but then the orderly lines of boys dissolved into what looked horribly like a mob. The crowd parted to let their leader through.

'I'm Alf, fen scum. *I'm* the solo voice here.' It was the big, spotty lad who'd stared at him so intently before. 'Think you're special, eh?'

Pip shook his head and took a step back. The boy was much bulkier than he was, and looked as if he could easily do him some serious damage. Perfect must have felt Pip's fear, for she stirred uneasily inside his tunic.

Unfortunately, the movement did not go unnoticed.

'He's got an animal with him!' one of the boys squealed. 'In his shirt – I saw it move!'

'Nay, that's just the fleas trying to get away – they can't stand the smell,' sneered Alf. 'Everybody knows fen folk stink. They can't help it, though – it's 'cause they have the pig in bed with them nights for fear it might wander off and drown.' And he did a very bad impression of a dying pig, flailing his hands about like trotters and snorting. The other boys laughed dutifully.

'All happy? That's grand. Now come on!'

The Precentor had appeared in the nick of time. He opened a little door in the great left hand one and scurried through. With a glower over his shoulder at Pip, Alf followed him, and the rest of the choir filed in behind, leaving Pip standing alone.

But just at the last minute one of the smaller boys nipped back to him and whispered, 'Don't mind him. Is it a pet? Do you *really* know Abbot Michael? We're not allowed pets. Could I see it? Later, maybe? But you'd better put it away somewhere for now, you know – it really isn't right to take a beast into the church. Eh?' before scampering nervously after the others again.

Pip looked about desperately for somewhere to hide Perfect – it would be just like that Alf to tell the Precentor on him! As far as it being *right* for a gargoyle to be in a church – well, where else would they be?!

Which gave him an idea.

'Quick, Perfect,' he whispered urgently. 'While nobody's looking!'

Perfect trickled down his sleeve and sat on his hand with her tail hanging down.

'I was scared,' she said woefully.

'Never mind,' Pip shushed her. 'But we need to hide you now . . . Look, see that bit up where the roof meets the wall? There in the corner? That looks to me as if it's just crying out for a gargoyle. A small one . . .'

Perfect twisted her head right round on her neck, spotted the corner, and twisted back to grin up at him.

'Perfect!' she said, and launched . . . just as another of the boys came back.

'What was that – a bat?' he said and then forgot about it. 'Hurry up – the Precentor wants you in the front row.'

Pip drew a ragged breath, and followed him inside.

Perfect's Dream

It was cold in the great Porch, but Perfect didn't mind. She was glad to be able to stretch herself and unkink her tail after hiding in Pip's tunic for so long. There are a number of standard gargoyle positions, and she settled immediately into one of the most strung-out, locked her claws, sighed contentedly, and fell asleep.

Time passed. The sound of the choir drifted faintly through the thick doors. Then, for a long while, there was quiet. The wind got up a little, and whined round the stones. And Perfect began to dream. She dreamed she heard voices, furtive, urgent voices. *Go away*, she thought crossly. *I'm asleep!* But they didn't go away. They just went on whispering – and then she suddenly felt an overpowering desire to sneeze. There was smoke tickling her nostrils – she could feel her front claws beginning to unlock so she could give her snout a good rub – *and why shouldn't I?* she thought blearily, and opened her eyes.

The burning torch one of the men held was almost directly underneath her, and the foul-smelling smoke made her want to cough. One of them was wearing a black floppy hat with a feather, and the other was a clergyman of some sort. She didn't recognise either of them, but that wasn't surprising. Humans tended to all look pretty much alike to Perfect, unless of course they were Pip.

One of the men was still speaking, loudly enough now for Perfect to hear his words.

'I've done everything I can think of to win the brat over,' he complained. 'I chose the cleanest, least disgusting beggars I could find for the Washing of the Feet. My choir is the best in England – I made sure he knew *that*, since you tell me he's supposed to care about music. I've given him the best fare I can get away with during Lent – the finest barnacle geese, best beaver steaks, my own private wines . . . You know I have no particular like for children, and

I have found my dealings with *this* one distasteful in the extreme!'

'Your Grace, you have been a saint.' The other man's voice oozed sincerity. 'And the boy's cousin is *not* a child – yet *another* reason to prefer him as our monarch.'

'Yes, yes, I know all that – but I can*not* have the boy killed in Ely. I would be suspected at once,' hissed the first man.

Perfect froze.

'*Not*, Your Grace, if the suspicion is already firmly placed *elsewhere*,' the second man murmured soothingly, though there was impatience too in his voice, as if he had explained all this many times before.

'So you *say*. May I remind you, however, that I have a great deal more to lose than you do, my Lord.'

'It's not a competition, Your Grace – we *are* on the same side! And may I remind *you* how much we both stand to *gain*? With Arnald out of the way, and his cousin on the throne, we will be the most powerful men in the kingdom. As things stand, the Bishop of London has a stranglehold on *everything*, but with this' – and he took something from his clothes and held it out in the palm of his hand –

'with *this*, we can change all that.'

The two men stared at the object in silence for a moment – and so did Perfect. It was a small glass bottle that glinted dully in the torchlight. If it had been a venomous snake or a hangman's noose he held in his hand, it could not have looked more sinister.

Suddenly, somewhere in the depths of the cathedral, a door slammed. The torch flickered madly for a moment in the wind, sending up a cloud of blinding, stinging smoke. Perfect squeezed her eyes shut and longed to lick them with her tongue. When she could see again, the torch and the two men were gone.

With a tiny whimper that no one heard, Perfect clung in the darkness and longed for Pip.

Chapter 11

Too Many Questions

The next twenty-four hours were unreal, desperate, exhilarating, awful. Singing with the Cathedral choir was amazing – in spite of Alf's continuing jibes about pig-boys and fen rats. But there was also the burden of what Perfect had overheard to carry. Pip *had* to tell someone – but who *could* he tell?

Who would believe him?

They knew one of the plotters was the Bishop, because Perfect had heard the other man call him 'Your Grace'. And they knew the other man was a noble because of being called 'my Lord'. But *which* noble? Ely was hooching with visiting lords.

'Would you recognise his voice again?' Pip asked.

Perfect shook her head. 'Not talking normally. They were whispering, don't forget, and whispers all sound alike.'

'But you'd know if you *saw* him?'

'Well . . . maybe. I'd only really know his hat. I'd know *that* again if I saw it – it was a black floppy hat with a big feather. So, as long as I'm looking down on him from above and he's wearing his hat and whispering and it's dark, I'm *sure* I would recognise him. Well, pretty sure.'

It wasn't much of a starting point, but it was all they had. Pip used every scrap of spare time he had trying to learn more. He eavesdropped shamelessly and then asked questions to fill in the gaps. Luckily there was no shortage of people who were eager to gossip. And though there were plenty of noblemen dancing attendance on the King for the gossip to be about, *two names* kept coming up again and again, more than any others.

Sir Robert.

And Sir Giles.

'Who are they? What are they like?' Pip would ask, trying to sound like a country bumpkin and succeeding very well. And then he'd be told! How one was a saint and the other was a devil in disguise. How one was generous to all, and the other was the meanest man in the kingdom. How one even killed a servant in a fit of rage and the other had saved a child from drowning in a flooding river . . .

There were as many stories as there were people telling them, and sometimes it was Sir Giles who was the hero and sometimes it was Sir Robert. The only thing everyone agreed on, was that Sir Giles was a handsome man and Sir Robert . . . wasn't.

By the end of the Saturday afternoon, Pip was a very confused nervous wreck.

'Somebody's going to start getting suspicious about this,' he murmured to Perfect. 'They're going to start wondering why I'm so curious.'

All Pip wanted to do was curl up in an unnoticed corner somewhere and *not think*. He'd completely lost track of time, as well, and it was just beginning to occur to him that it might be getting late, when—

'*There he is!*' said an angry voice, a hand landed on his shoulder, and he shut his eyes and screamed.

The Lady Chapel

'What's wrong, child? Has someone frightened you?'

Pip opened his eyes and stared into Brother John's kindly face.

'There's no *time* for that now, Brother. We've wasted too much of it just locating the . . . him.' It was Prior Benet. He looked as if he'd bitten into something sour, and then been told he wasn't allowed to spit it out.

'You're right, of course, Brother,' said Brother John amiably. 'Come along, Pip – we must hurry, and I can tell all about it as we go.'

'G-go?' stuttered Pip.

Prior Benet muttered something under his

breath, but Brother John put an arm round Pip's shoulders and drew him gently along.

'It's sinful, of course it is, to rejoice at some one else's misfortune, and he seems a perfectly nice boy, and it will have been a terrible shock to him – though not a *surprise* really, since he must have known it would happen, because that's the way God made us, after all, and who are we to argue with His design, even when some things do seem a little, well, *unnecessary*—'

'Will you come to the point?!' grated the Prior.

'Ah . . . yes . . . I'm sorry, Brother . . .'

The Prior grabbed Pip from Brother John and hustled him along at a much brisker pace.

'The boy who was to have sung the solo at the King's service tonight can't because his voice broke, just like that, just today.' The Prior's tone seemed to suggest the boy had done it on purpose, simply to inconvenience everyone. 'And Brother Mark the Precentor wants *you*' – that sour expression was back on his face in full force, Pip noticed – 'to sing it instead. But you couldn't be found! The service starts any minute now, if we're not already too late . . .'

Most of Pip's brain had closed down, but

a bit of it couldn't help but enjoy the Prior's discomfort.

'You'll sing it beautifully,' Brother John was saying to him now, encouraging, smiling. 'I know you'll make us proud, lad. Though' – and his face creased anxiously – 'of *course* pride is a sin' – then the creases cleared – 'still I'm sure, this once, God would understand . . .'

They had caught up with the choir now, and a novice pounced on Pip. He caught a brief glimpse of Alf's stricken face – then a white surplice was thrown over his head, an ornate candlestick was thrust into his hands, and he was shoved into place just as the procession began.

Through the numb terror that filled him, Pip was just aware of Perfect working her way round inside his tunic and then slithering down the inside of his sleeve. She waited until the lighter had touched Pip's candle with his taper and then emerged to wrap herself quickly round the candlestick, blending with the decorative carving.

Pip was shaking so badly, hot wax from the candle began to spatter painfully onto his hands. Perfect licked it off his skin as fast as her tongue would go – it was real beeswax, not the cheap lard candles of Wickit, and no hardship at all for a gargoyle to eat, but she was *mostly* doing it to be kind. She left the spatters on her own stone skin to cool, and when Pip looked down she was sporting a pointy wax hat between her ears that dribbled down the side of her face in a jaunty fashion, with a blob on the end a bit like a tassel or a pom-pom.

She looked so adorably ridiculous that Pip's numbness melted a little – down to about the level of enormous fear. Perfect must have been able to sense the change, because she risked a wink and a tiny claws-up of encouragement as the procession reached the cathedral doors, and stopped.

The Precentor was trotting fussily along the line, straightening a surplice on one boy, offering a quick word of encouragement to another, like a pint sized general inspecting his troops before battle.

Then he came to Pip.

He took a moment to put a hand on the boy's shoulder and look him in the eyes. Then he smiled and leaned closer, so just the two of them could hear.

'What did he teach you, eh? Our good friend Michael – what were his words? Did he say to you, *Aim, boy, aim?*' The Precentor's attempt at a Welsh accent was terrible, but suddenly Pip could hear his

Abbot speaking and it warmed the cold stone in his throat a little more. He nodded and managed a small smile.

And Brother Mark moved on down his lines of troops to the end, then sounded the pitch as the great doors opened, and the procession moved off, following the cross out of the dying day and into the blazing expanse of the Cathedral.

The choir paused under the great Octagon and split to let the Bishop and the royal party pass through ahead of them.

And Pip was hit by a sudden wave of doubt. The Bishop of Ely was an imposing sight as he strode forward, every inch the embodiment of God's authority. Already unusually tall, he was made to seem even taller by the satin mitre on his head. He wore silk vestments thick with embroidery and jewels that flashed in the candlelight. He carried a mighty crozier, heavy with carving and precious stones, thumping it down every few steps and swinging it forward again as if its weight were nothing to him. It was impossible to believe that such a one could be involved in anything petty or human or evil.

And then Pip saw his face and began to doubt his doubt. It was a cruel face, with hard scowling lines around the mouth and deeply etched marks between his eyebrows. It was a face that expected absolute submission and would allow no leeway. There was something about the Bishop's eyes, something that reminded him suddenly of Patrick Jerome, the pike.

First the predator, and then the prey. The King followed on, dressed in the finest black brocade. He wore a fortune on his back, and he held himself with a casual arrogance, sure of his own importance. Compared to most people, he would have looked pretty impressive. But compared to the *Bishop* . . . To Pip, Arnald looked suddenly vulnerable. Vulnerable and small.

And then, directly behind, came the rival nobles Pip had been hearing about all day. The one called Sir Giles walked easily, his fair hair beautifully groomed, his hands behind his back, a look of devotion on his handsome face. Beside him, Sir Robert looked awkward and bad-tempered. His black eyes were never still, flicking back and forth suspiciously at the crowds. And he held, twisted between clenched hands, a floppy hat.

A black floppy hat with a large feather.

Perfect squeaked audibly, and at once the black eyes zeroed in. Pip pretended to clear his throat, as if *he'd* made the noise, and the moment passed. White-faced, he glanced down at Perfect. Her eyes were huge and her mouth was making a silent 'Oooo. . .' shape.

Then the boy beside him gave him a shove. The choir reformed and turned into the Processional Way. Pip's brain was whirling so fast he could barely remember to breathe. What should he do? There was nothing he could do. He *must* do something . . .

Then they entered the Lady Chapel and suddenly, he forgot everything else.

Like the rest of the Cathedral, the Lady Chapel had been stripped of its draperies and decorations to mark the time of Jesus' death. But Pip didn't notice any lack. All he could see was light, and height, and soaring windows of glass, and the dance of saints and apostles carved round the walls.

And then the singing began.

Pip had no knowledge of acoustics, but the builders of the Lady Chapel *did*. Every note had a special resonance, every word was clear and rich. He couldn't pay attention to anything else. As the high and mighty listened and the night outside fell, Pip sang his heart out and the room gave it back ten times over.

It was all finished much too quickly. Pip felt shuddery and numb at the same time as he followed the rest of the choir out through the Monks' Door and into the cloister. Some of the boys had given him nods of approval and Brother Mark beamed at him in passing. Pip tried to smile back, but found instead he was, astonishingly, close to tears. He thrust his candlestick at the nearest boy (Perfect was safely back inside his tunic by this time, a reassuring lump) and ran.

When he stopped running, Pip found he had ended up in the tangle of corridors and storerooms behind the guest quarters. He opened a door at random and, nicking a torch from its bracket, stumbled inside. He slumped down on the floor.

'What are we going to do?' he wailed quietly.

Perfect crept out from his tunic and perched herself on his knee.

'Well,' she said. 'I'd have thought that was obvious. Now we know who the bad guys are, we go and give the King fair warning.'

'But *how*?!' Pip groaned. 'He's not exactly staying in the Guest Hall, is he, and he's sure to be surrounded by guards, and there's no way they'd let someone like *me* in for a chat and . . . Perfect, are you *listening* to me?!'

The gargoyle didn't answer. She was staring intently at a shelf.

'Perfect?'

Pip felt her tense, then launch awkwardly in the confined space. For a moment she teetered on the edge of the shelf, then grabbed hold of the handle of a big jug, and wrapped herself round it.

'That King Person can't lick himself clean with such a sad little tongue,' she said. 'Don't you think we should take the poor grubby wee king some nice hot water to wash in? Hmmm?'

The Royal Rooms

No one in the kitchen looked twice at Pip when he asked for hot water. With so many noble guests staying, there were all sorts of strangers coming and going about their masters' business. It took a while to find his way to the Bishop's extensive quarters, but at last he came to a grand corridor – and at the end of it was a door guarded by two armed men.

Pip walked towards them, trying to look confident. If only he could stop his hands shaking . . .

One of the guards seemed prepared to ignore him completely, but the other was clearly in the mood for throwing his weight around. And his weight was considerable. He was *huge* and he had hands like great hairy slabs of meat and he smelled of beer.

'And just where do you think *you're* going?!' he growled. 'WELL?! *What are you here for?*'

Pip's voice seemed to have completely deserted him. With an enormous effort, he managed to squeak, 'I . . . I . . .' before it disappeared again.

'I would have thought it was *obvious* where the boy is going, and what he's here for,' said a voice suddenly. 'And if the King's washing water has got cold, I'll just tell him why, shall I?'

It was Sir Giles. He had come up behind Pip unnoticed and was standing there looking relaxed and pleasant. But the guard's red face turned pale at the sight of him. He tried to salute, bow, drag the door open and apologise all at the same time. Pip was amazed.

'*Hugh*, isn't it,' said Sir Giles. 'You're one of *my* men, aren't you.'

'Yes, sir. Your-your humble servant, sir!'

'I hope so, *Hugh* . . . for your sake.'

The nobleman gestured to Pip to carry on into the room, and then followed behind him, drawing the door gently to.

Pip turned to thank Sir Giles – and caught a

glimpse of a strange expression on the nobleman's face. It was gone in an instant, but even so . . . for a second there was a look of leering pleasure on Sir Giles' face, as if he'd really enjoyed humiliating that guard. Then it was gone, and he was all smiles again.

Pip shook his head a little, sure he must be mistaken. Perfect gave her head a tiny shake too, but whether that was because she'd seen something too, or was just warning him not to stand there like a lump, he couldn't tell.

Moving carefully, he made his way to a table by the wall and set down the tray. He fiddled with the jug and towel for a minute . . . now he was here, he had no idea what to do next!

What now?! he mouthed at Perfect, who shrugged her shoulder and pulled a face.

You're a big help, he thought, looking about desperately for inspiration – which was when he noticed the mirror.

It was small, with a curvy wooden frame, and it bowed in the middle, so he had a sort of fish-eyed view of practically the entire room. He'd never come across anything like it – he'd never seen *any* sort of mirror before, and this was fascinating, the way he could see the tiny figures moving about, like a living picture. It took only the slightest movement of his head to bring different corners and bits of furniture into view. He could see the royal bed with its elaborately embroidered spread and heavy curtains. He could see the King, standing there sullenly in his nightshirt while Sir Robert was obviously giving him some sort of lecture in a low voice. He could see Sir Giles, courteously waiting his turn, standing by another table where the King's supper was laid out. He could see the gold plates and the delicious food and the wine goblets and jug. He could see Sir Giles reach casually into his tunic, bring out a little glass bottle and pour it into a goblet, before adding some wine. Pip blinked hard, and peered wildly into the mirror . . . which was when he saw a thing that made his brain spin. Sir Giles had something with him that Pip hadn't noticed before. He stared, open-mouthed, as the nobleman set the something casually down on a chair.

It was a hat. A black, floppy hat, with a long feather.

Suddenly everything shifted and cleared in Pip's mind, like a shape in the mist when the wind comes up – all at once he was seeing the real thing, and not just guessing.

It was *Sir Giles* who wanted to kill the King, *not* Sir Robert!

'Now, Your Majesty, I suggest you go and wash,' said Sir Robert, raising his voice. 'The boy has brought you water, and your meal is ready.'

'Or, you could just come over here, and have a cup of wine!' Sir Robert stiffened at the sound of Sir Giles' voice. Arnald smirked – it was clear he was smarting from his telling-off, and welcomed a chance for a little defiance. He strutted over to the dining table and took the cup from the smiling Sir Giles.

Sir Robert didn't react, however. He went to the window instead and gazed out into the night. Arnald looked sulky.

'I'm going to wash now,' he said and carried the goblet, untasted, over to where Pip was standing. He put it down beside the basin. Glancing up, he caught sight of Pip staring at him, wild-eyed, in the mirror. The King frowned.

'Just a minute,' he said. 'I know you! You're the boy who sang in the service, aren't you? *You're* not a servant – what are you doing here?'

Pip's face went white, but fortunately, neither of the noblemen appeared to have heard anything. Sir Robert was still staring out of the window, and

Sir Giles had picked up his hat again and was elegantly smoothing the feather. Pip half-raised his hand to shush the other boy, before remembering just who it was he was telling to keep it down.

Arnald frowned. 'What's the matter with you?!' he demanded. If anything, his voice was even *louder* this time.

In desperation, Pip pointed at the goblet, then at Arnald, and then grabbed his own throat and pretended to strangle himself. The King's frown only deepened, so Pip did it again, crossing his eyes and letting his tongue hang out in an attempt to represent somebody dying.

Arnald took a step back – he must have thought Pip was going mad – and started to turn his head to call for help, when the sound of a small, cross voice from the level of the table made him freeze.

'Stop being so stupid, King,' the voice said. 'He's trying to tell you – the wine's poisoned!'

Chapter 14

Demons and Dwale

The King looked down. There was Perfect, squatting on her hind legs, her front paws on her hips, her tail tapping the table impatiently. Arnald's eyes grew huge with horror, and he made a sign against the evil eye.

'*God save us!*' he whispered. 'Are – are you a *demon*?! From h-hell?'

Perfect tutted crossly. 'Of *course* not! I'm part of a *church*, for heaven's sake! I'm very probably a lot holier than *you* are, Master Anointed King Person, if you want to get competitive about it. But you don't have time – we're *telling* you you're in mortal danger – the wine's been poisoned by the smiling chap behind you. We've done *our* bit, so now, what are *you* going to do?'

But Arnald seemed to be having trouble coming to grips with being scolded by a bit of architecture.

'Er . . .' was all he managed to say.

'Your Majesty,' murmured Pip. 'You must trust us. I don't understand why they want you dead, but it's God's truth. Perfect heard them – Sir Giles and the Bishop – plotting in the Cathedral. And I saw Sir Giles, just now, in the mirror, *do* it . . . put the poison into the cup.'

The King looked up then at the images in the mirror, and was quiet for a long moment. Then, still staring into the mirror, he picked up the goblet and held it out. Pip jerked the washing bowl into position and the King tipped the cup and poured. The wine rippled there for a moment, sending red fingers out into the clear water, looking like blood. There was a brief, bitter smell. Then it was still.

'A pleasant vintage, my Lord,' said Arnald suddenly. It made Pip and Perfect both jump, but the comment was directed over his shoulder. He was watching Sir Giles in the mirror now, and did not miss the look of smug satisfaction that flitted across the nobleman's face.

'Our friend the Bishop would hardly offer you less than his best, Your Majesty.' And he put a hand up before his mouth to hide a smile. You could still see it in his eyes, though.

Sir Giles *was* feeling pretty pleased with the world in general, and himself in particular. But there was no time to lose – he had to get himself out of the room and safely away before the poison began to take effect. No one could possibly blame *him* for the young King's so sad, so unexpected demise . . . He edged toward the door.

Pip was thinking, *So handsome, so charming – it's all been just an act. It's the power he cares about, not the people. Like that guard at the door* . . . He glanced over at Arnald.

The young King's face was white and strained. *He'd* been trusting Sir Giles for months. And unlike the guard on the door, it wasn't just his *job* the nobleman was threatening to take away. Pip thought Arnald did well to stay so in control of himself – he thought, *how would I feel if it turned out that Brother Barnard, say, actually hated me, hated me so much he wanted me dead.* But then he realised it wasn't like that. Sir Giles didn't hate the King – he didn't feel anything about him at all. Arnald was nothing – just an obstacle, like a chair or a dog when you wanted to cross a room, and it was in the way. And unlike Brother Barnard, Sir Giles was clever. Frighteningly clever. And any moment now, he was going to start wondering what they were up to . . .

'Pretend to have a thirst,' whispered Pip.

'What?'

'That bitter smell – I'm sure it's belladonna. And if it *is* what he put in your wine, a great thirst is one of the signs! Say you're thirsty!' It was all Pip could do not to scream at him. 'Ask him for more drink!'

Arnald cocked an eyebrow. 'He's a Lord of the Realm – not a skivvy!'

Pip made a strangled noise.

'He means, *get on with it!*' Perfect translated. The tip of her tail had started to jerk about nervously as if it were trying to escape from the rest of her.

Arnald nodded, but still hesitated. 'I don't think . . .' he whispered, looking from Perfect to Pip. 'Shouldn't it be hidden . . . ?'

'*It?!*' Perfect squawked, but Pip stuck out his arm. 'Not *now*, Perfect!' he muttered, and hustled her up his sleeve.

Arnald took a deep breath, pretended to dry his face on the towel and, still muffled, turned round.

'The Bishop's wine has given me such a thirst, Sir Giles,' he said. 'Will you pour me another cup? Oh, must you leave?'

Arnald dropped the towel on the floor and strolled across to the table. Sir Giles had almost reached the door by this point.

'Sadly, Your Majesty, I must,' he replied, with only the slightest tremor in his voice to suggest any nervousness.

'Never mind, Sir Giles – the boy can do it. There's no need for you to serve me yourself, though' – and Arnald glared grumpily at Sir Robert – 'it *is* pleasant to have such amiable company.'

Sir Giles made him an elaborate bow.

'You are too kind, Your Majesty. But I will be gone for only a short time and then' – and he shot a hard look at Sir Robert – 'then I will most assuredly be back.'

Arnald inclined his head graciously, and Sir Giles, hat in hand, was free to go.

As soon as the door shut behind him, Sir Robert was across the room in two steps and had Pip by the throat.

'Talk, boy!' he barked. 'What have you been threatening the King with?'

Pip was thunderstruck.

'What . . . How . . . ?!' he croaked.

'It's not *him*, Sir Robert!' Arnald was trying to pull him off Pip. 'He came to *warn* me. It's *Sir Giles* . . . !'

Sir Robert let go reluctantly.

'*Sir Giles?!*' he growled. 'Explain yourself!'

Pip, rubbing his throat, pointed at the stained water in the bowl and gasped, 'He was trying to poison the King. I . . . I overheard him plotting . . . with the Bishop . . . so I came . . .'

Sir Robert fixed him with a hard gaze, as if to read his heart, and then nodded, satisfied.

'You came and got throttled for your trouble. Your pardon, lad. I was watching you in the reflection in the window and it all seemed . . . suspicious.'

Pip and Arnald exchanged alarmed glances – had he seen Perfect?

It would seem not, for the nobleman continued without pause. 'Now,' he said, 'you must tell me everything you know, and quickly! You heard him say he'd be back soon, and I wager he won't be alone this time!'

Chapter 15

Sir Robert Makes a Mess

'Poison the King and make sure somebody else takes the blame . . . That'd be me, then,' said Sir Robert ruefully. 'The clever little . . . and having *done* it – he *thinks* – all he has to do now is break in here with a dozen guards at his back and find *me*, alone with a dead king on my hands. He could skewer me on the spot and get away with it. There'd be nobody to say anything different!'

'There'd be me,' protested Pip.

Sir Robert snorted. '*You* don't count,' he said. 'Besides—' and he made a slitting gesture across his throat. 'Work of a moment.'

'I can't believe that Sir Giles . . .' began Arnald, and then stopped. He was suddenly white-faced and starting to shake. Pip had seen signs like that before in Brother Gilbert's infirmary, when those with wounds or broken bones had been brought in. He led Arnald closer to the fire and looked anxiously over at Sir Robert. The nobleman nodded, pulled a leather flask from his tunic, unstoppered it and thrust it under the King's nose.

'Here, drink this.'

Arnald reared back, horrified, but Sir Robert put a firm hand on his shoulder.

'Don't worry,' he said gruffly. 'It's not poisoned.'

Arnald shuddered, then took the flask and drank.

'Good,' said Sir Robert encouragingly. 'Now . . . we're agreed the scoundrel's clever. His plan *should* have worked. But he's not the only one who can plot and scheme. And if we're quick about it, I think we can present just as convincing a story as his!'

'What are you going to do?' It was Arnald. He was a better colour now.

'Get you safely out of here, for starters.'

'But how . . . ?'

Sir Robert rubbed his chin speculatively. 'I would say that a band of armed men is going to break in, kidnap you and drag you off into the night. *I* will do everything humanly possible to keep this from happening, of course, but I'll be overpowered and found unconscious and bleeding on the floor.'

He was confronted by two blank faces. He sighed and turned to Pip.

'Look, imagine you and the King here are baby ducks. When the heron threatens a family of ducklings, what happens?'

Pip could only stare, amazed.

'What happens?!' Sir Robert barked.

Pip jumped and stuttered, 'They – they dive, my Lord, the little ones, down to the bottom. And the mother flaps about, disturbing the surface of the water with her wings so the heron can't see where they are . . . OH! You're going to flap, my Lord, aren't you, while we dive!'

Sir Robert grinned, suddenly looking years younger.

'Now, a band of armed men would not want to be disturbed too soon, so first' – and he started to drag a heavy chest towards the door – 'they'd make a barricade.'

Arnald jumped up.

'But wait – how will we get out?'

'Same way the royal piss-pot gets out.'

'What?!'

Pip could hear him chuckle as he pushed the chest hard against the door. Then he straightened.

'Over there.'

You had to look carefully, but once you knew where it was you could see the outline of a small door in the wall. It was over in the corner where a discreet screen had been set up. This was where the King's potty resided.

'Never wonder where it went after you filled it?'

Arnald reddened but lifted his chin stubbornly and said nothing.

Sir Robert ignored him. 'Now – the struggle,' he murmured, and walking over to the bed, he calmly took hold of the curtains and ripped them down with a sudden violent jerk.

Pip backed away nervously . . . and knocked over a chair.

'That's the spirit,' said Sir Robert.

Then they all helped, until the room looked like a convincing battlefield.

'Enough fun,' said Sir Robert. 'Now, me.'

He drew his knife and cut himself

quickly, three times – on the forearm, on the thigh, and a nick to the ear.

'Ears bleed a lot,' he said. 'I want to be able to spread it around.' He proceeded to do so, adding more rips to his clothing while he was at it.

By the time he was finished, Sir Robert looked as if he really *had* been at the receiving end of a vicious attack.

'And then, to top it all, I've been knocked out,' he said, lying down on the floor and adopting a dramatic, limbs-flung-about pose. 'Good. And now, my ducklings, dive!' He lifted his head. 'And don't tell *anyone* where!'

Now it had come to it, Pip realised he had no idea where to go.

'But . . . '

'*Not anyone!* In case all this' – and he waved a hand round at the mess – 'doesn't work.'

Both boys gulped audibly.

'*GET OUT!!*' roared Sir Robert.

Pip nearly jumped out of his skin. He grabbed Arnald, dragged him through the little door and banged it shut behind them.

In the sudden dark, he stopped, unable to think anything but, *Now what? Now what? Now what?* over and over again.

Then Perfect's little voice sounded in the black.

'Pip?' she said.

'Y-yes?'

'Let's go home.'

Chapter 16

Into the Night

It was a good idea, and it gave Pip new heart.

'Right, Your Majesty,' he said. 'We're going to Wickit. You'll be safe there.'

'Wickit? Never heard of it.'

'No, Sire. Let's hope Sir Giles hasn't either.'

It wasn't long before they found a door that opened into a tiny lane behind the Bishop's quarters.

Pip shook his head impatiently. 'This is no good – I can't tell where we are.'

'Turn left,' said Perfect.

'Because . . . ?'

'Because then you have a fifty-fifty chance of being right . . . er, correct.'

Pip snorted scornfully, but turned left anyway. Then, at the same moment, he and Perfect both said, 'Ah!' They had come out not far from the kitchens, and the bulk of the Cathedral loomed beyond.

'Now for the pier!' began Pip, but Perfect thought otherwise.

'You can't take the boy through the streets like that!' she said.

Pip skidded to a stop.

Arnald was shivering again. Sir Robert had insisted he leave in just his nightshirt and slippers – 'Armed villains are hardly going to stand about politely while you choose an outfit, Your Majesty,' he said firmly. 'You'd be dragged away as you stand.'

After the heat of the state bedroom with its roaring fire, the night air was piercing.

The royal teeth chattered audibly.

'I – I beg your pardon, Your Highness. You must be cold.'

Perfect snorted.

'Yes, well, more *importantly*, he's going to stick out like a white crow on the streets. Correct me if I'm wrong, but it's not exactly *normal*, what he's wearing, is it? And we are trying to go *unnoticed*, aren't we?'

'Your pet has a point,' said the King. (He didn't even notice Perfect's indignant gasp.) 'Servants' clothes would be best. Something someone unimportant might wear. What you're wearing would do.'

He honestly looked as if he expected Pip to strip off on the spot.

'I guess you could use my old clothes,' said Pip. 'They're in a bundle by my bed in the Guest Hall.' There was a doorway nearby, and he hurried Arnald into its shadow. 'Wait here – I'll be as quick as I can!'

But rumour is faster than anything on two legs. By the time Pip got to the Guest Hall, people were already gathering in little groups, exchanging urgent whispers and looking over their shoulders suspiciously. Pip was desperate to know what they were all saying, but he was even more desperate not to be held up. Fortunately, the friendly merchants hadn't come back to the Guest Hall yet, and no one else paid any attention to an insignificant boy. Heart pounding, Pip picked up his bundle and walked out again.

'Got 'em!' he announced triumphantly as he rejoined the King in the doorway.

But it was clear the minute he held them up

that his old clothes were much too small for the other boy. There was nothing for it – Pip would have to give Arnald his new clothes and go back to wearing the old ones. He wasn't happy about it.

But then, neither was the King.

'This *itches*!' whined Arnald. 'How can you expect me to wear anything so scratchy – what did you do – make them out of hedgehog quills?! And they *smell*!'

Pip sniffed. 'I can't smell anything,' he said.

'They smell like ten wet sheep and they feel like one hundred dead hedgehogs and if you say there's nothing wrong with them you're a liar!'

'There's nothing wrong with them,' Pip muttered sullenly to himself. And inside his head he was shouting, *Those are my new clothes, the first set of **new clothes** I've ever had and if I had my choice **I wouldn't let you near them** but we don't have any choice. Do we. **Your Majesty**.*

'What terrible manners!' Perfect stuck her head out of Pip's old hood and tutted. 'Would you rather we didn't save your life, then?'

Arnald looked down at his satin house shoes (both Pip's old *and* new shoes were too small to fit the royal feet) and then, sulkily, he shook his head.

'Right. Let's go,' said Perfect and, without looking at each other, the two boys set off.

The trip through the town was hair-raising. They ran down the dark streets, expecting to hear a hue-and-cry at their heels every moment. Unrest seemed to be spreading out from the monastery buildings in expanding circles, like ripples on a black pond.

'Hey! You there! Where do you think you're going?'

A burly man loomed suddenly out of a doorway, making both boys squeal in fright. Pip grabbed the King's arm and dragged him down a side-alley, squelching through smelly muck and dodging piles of rubbish. Fortunately for them, the big man wasn't as agile. They heard him go down with a roar and some quite creative cursing.

'This way,' whispered Pip. 'Come on!'

It seemed to take forever, but somehow they made it as far as the town wall without further incident. Panting, they huddled out of sight in the cold shadows by the gate.

'Wait here – I'll take a quick look ahead.'

Perfect launched herself from Pip's shoulder. The two boys stared after her.

'I'll give you a bag of gold for her,' said Arnald, suddenly. '*And* a bag of silver.'

'Shut up!' muttered Pip. In spite of the perishing night, he felt hot now all over. *How **dare** he?!* An anger demon began to dance in his head and his hands clenched into fists. *How dare he try to buy Perfect?! One more word out of him, just one more word, and I'll punch his face in* . . .

'And this ring,' said Arnald. He hadn't noticed the expression on Pip's face.

The next instant, Arnald was sitting on his royal backside in the mud.

'*You hit me!*' he gasped. 'You hit your king!'

'You deserved it – and a lot more!' Pip was past caring. 'You're arrogant, and rude, and selfish, and . . . and . . . pig-headed. And rude.'

'You already said that,' said Arnald. 'You said rude twice.'

'That's because you're twice as rude as anybody I've ever met in my whole life – and that includes bloody Prior Benet!'

'Is he awful?'

'*Awful?!* You would not *believe* how awful he is. He's as awful as . . . as an eel-pie full of maggots.

And so are you. So there.' Pip's fury was running down now. It never lasted long.

Arnald pulled himself up, and wiped the blood from his nose.

'Maggoty eel-pie, eh?' he said. 'You know who you sound like? Sir Robert. He's always telling me off.'

Pip shuffled uncomfortably. 'I wish *he* were here.'

Arnald heaved a sigh. 'Yes. Me too.'

At that moment, Perfect returned.

'Okay,' she said. 'Looks like nobody's about – what happened to *you*?!' she squeaked, noticing Arnald's bloody nose.

Both boys looked embarrassed.

'I . . . tripped,' muttered the King.

'I hit him,' admitted Pip.

Perfect looked disgusted, then dived back into Pip's hood.

Pip and Arnald slipped through the gateway and huddled for a moment in the lee of the wall. The buildings around the pier and along the shoreline were not much more than shacks. Sounds of merriment spilled out briefly, along with a splash of light as someone opened a door to look out. But they shut it again almost at once.

The pier was a strip of darkness that reached out into the moving black of the water. Punts were tied up along its length, and they could hear them bumping uneasily against each other as the wind shifted them about. It was a cold night, with a threat of snow in the air. Everyone who could be was staying indoors, in the warm.

'Let's go,' said Pip.

The wood of the pier was wet and slick, and glinted weirdly in a brief glimpse of moonlight from between the clouds. Both boys slithered as they hurried forward.

'There!' said Pip, pointing. 'That's ours.'

As he held the Wickit boat steady for Arnald, a thought hit him suddenly – right out of nowhere – that Brother John and Prior Benet would have no idea what had happened to him – and no way of getting home again! *They'll think I stole the punt!* thought Pip, appalled. *Or Prior Benet will, anyway. And Brother John will think something awful has happened . . .*

Then he looked down at the huddled, miserable figure of the boy King, and thought, *Something awful **has** happened.*

The pole came reluctantly out of the mud with an enormous slurping sound. Both boys crouched, sure someone would have heard – but there was nothing. No doors banging open, no floods of light, no angry shouts of, 'Stop thief!'

'Let's go,' hissed Arnald.

Pip pushed off, and tried not to wince at every splash and clunk. It seemed the more silent he tried to be, the clumsier he became – yet still their luck held.

Quarter of the way there. Half the way there . . .

Arnald was muttering in the middle of the boat.

'What are you *doing*?!' snapped Pip, irritated in spite of his panic.

'Praying the clouds don't clear,' was the answer.

Pip looked up, and swallowed, hard. The wind must have strengthened – the cloud cover was beginning to shred. If the moon came through while they were still in open water, they'd be clearly visible. He redoubled his efforts with the pole.

Perfect suddenly scrambled past him to the stern of the punt and stared anxiously back the way they'd come.

'Guards!' she hissed – and that was when their luck gave out.

Chapter 17

Pursued

The clouds had fled, and the Wickit punt and its occupants were lit by the full force of the moon. You'd have to be blind not to see them.

'Stop them - they've stolen the King!'

Pip risked a look back – then wished he hadn't.

The pier was swarming with armed men and townsfolk. (It was illegal for citizens not to join in on a manhunt, and doubly so when a king was involved!) Torches jerked about wildly as guards tried to run on the slippery surface. Orders and curses could be distinctly heard, and the clumping of punt poles against the sides of a dozen boats.

'Thank heaven there are no archers!' muttered Arnald.

I never even thought of that! Pip said to himself.

He could see the channel now, and he powered their punt towards it. Then, just as they were in amongst the reeds and out of sight of their pursuers, the moon went behind another cloud.

Arnald swore in a very unroyal fashion, and Pip barked at Perfect, 'I can't see – go up in the bow and guide me!'

'Is that because we don't want to risk a light?' said Arnald.

'It's because we don't *have* a light!' Pip grunted.

'Left! More left!' Perfect called back.

It was a nightmare that seemed to have no end. Pip took every side channel Perfect could spot, every twist and turn that would hide them from the chase. He couldn't hope to outrun them – he hadn't the strength – but in the dark there was a shadow of a chance the pursuers might pass them by without realising it.

Then, '*Stop!*' hissed Perfect.

Pip nudged the punt into some sedge, and struggled to quieten his breathing. He looked over at Arnald. His face was visible as a pale smudge in the murk. Pip leaned across and pulled his hood further forward, then did the same with his own.

'Got an idea!' whispered Perfect suddenly, and before anyone could stop her, she'd slipped over the side of the boat into the black water.

Arnald was shaking so hard their boat was starting to make tiny splashy sounds. Pip put a steadying hand on his shoulder.

The moments passed, and the sounds of the searchers drew closer and closer until . . .

'*What's that?*' The voice sounded as if it were right behind them.

'Look!' It was another voice, a bit further over. 'A light! We've got them!'

What?! thought Pip. He peered frantically about, straining his eyes in the darkness. Then, suddenly, he saw it too. A flickering light, not far off, low down in the black. Then it was gone.

'The fools lit a lantern!'

Pip shuddered. He knew that voice.

'Sir Giles!' whispered Arnald in horror.

Then another voice with a Fen burr to it spoke. 'No, my Lord. It's never a lantern. Or not a human one, anyway.' This man was afraid – *to argue with Sir Giles, he'd have to be **terrified**!* thought Pip. 'That's Will of the Wykes, my Lord.'

'What are you gibbering about? Get after them, man!'

'It's the Lantern Man, sir. It's death to follow him!'

Pip could practically *feel* Sir Giles' anger growing. 'Look – they've lit it again! It's further to the left now – *they're getting away!!*'

'No – my Lord – listen!' The fenman sounded desperate. 'The Lantern Man is a devil, sir – he'll lure you on till you're lost and then drag you under – he'll eat your flesh and steal your soul – you don't understand—'

Pip heard the unmistakable metallic slither of a sword being pulled from its sheath. Arnald must have heard it too – Pip felt him tense under his hand.

'Then you'd best ask yourself, scum of the marsh, what you fear *most.*'

There was a cry, as Sir Giles moved suddenly against the man.

'Next time it will be your throat, and not just your ugly face,' they heard him snarl. 'Now take us after them – THERE! I see it again! That way!'

In the end there was barely six feet of reeds between them and the pursuers. As the boats passed, Pip could see strange twisted shadows and shapes in the spurts of torchlight that broke through to them. They were so close he could hear the rasping breath of the wounded man, punting in pain towards one fear and carrying another along with him. It was impossible that they would be missed – but the impossible happened. The two boys held their breath in disbelief as the hunt was lured away into the darkness.

Then, just as the last shout faded, the moon drifted out from behind the clouds again. Arnald looked like drowned death in the flat light, and Pip knew he'd be the same.

'A few minutes sooner . . . ' Arnald shook his head.

'I know.' Pip felt numb inside.

'What *were* those lights!' asked Arnald, his eyes like black glinting stones in his face.

'They were me!' said a voice from the water.

Arnald reared back and almost fell out of the boat; Pip slammed a hand over his mouth to keep himself from screaming; and Perfect slithered over the gunwale, one big grin on legs.

'That was fun!' she announced, and started to lick the drips off her shoulder.

The boys stared at her.

'*You* were . . .?'

'How did you . . .?'

Perfect tried to look nonchalant for about a second, then gave in, hopped up on the seat, and told all.

'Pip, do you remember when those fishermen got fogged in at the monastery and had to stay the night? And they were supposed to sleep in the kitchen but instead they sat up for *ages*, telling stories, and you pretended to be asleep, but really we were listening to every word, until the Bad Brother came in and told them off, and one of the fishermen called him that rude word after he'd gone?'

Pip nodded.

'WELL, *one* of the stories was about–'

'. . . the Lantern Man!' exclaimed Pip. 'I remember! I was scared witless!'

Perfect shrugged smugly. 'Well, of course I wasn't, but tonight I thought, *Wouldn't it be handy if a Lantern Man showed up **now**!* And *then* I thought, *Hang on – who needs a Lantern Man when you've got **me**!*'

'But how—'

'It was easy! Here's me – swim, swim, swim – roll over on my back – *whoosh*!' She lay on her back and gave a demonstration flame, narrowly avoiding singeing the royal eyebrows. Arnald jerked back, and Pip peered round anxiously.

'Careful!' he warned, but Perfect just waved a paw.

'Don't worry – I led them well away! They won't find *us* again! I'd be surprised if they can find their way back to *Ely* this side of tomorrow noon!'

Pip reached over and rubbed the place between her ears.

'You are the cleverest gargoyle in all of England,' he said.

She didn't argue.

The third time Pip rammed them into the side of a floating island, the punt stuck. Fast.

'What do you mean, *stuck*?' demanded Arnald through chattering teeth.

'What do you *think* I mean?!' Pip snapped back. He wasn't cold – all the effort of punting had seen to that – but he was achingly weary. 'Not that it matters. We might as well be lost standing still as lost blundering about.'

Arnald made a small strangled noise.

'Well, what do you expect?!' Pip blustered. 'It's *dark*, in case you hadn't noticed, and we don't have a lantern, we don't have a torch, I can't see the sky so I can't steer by the stars, and the moon's been and set by now anyway!'

Arnald shifted a little on the hard bench. 'I didn't say a word,' he muttered.

Pip sagged. 'I know,' he said, flopping down opposite him. 'I guess I was just yelling at myself.' He heaved a big sigh. 'Doing Prior Benet's job for him, since he's not here to do it himself!'

'Nobody actually *yells* at me much,' said Arnald after a while. 'But Sir Robert can sure get a lot of disapproval across, even without it.' He shifted again. 'That man can certainly lecture!'

Pip thought for a minute. 'But maybe . . . maybe he lectures you 'cause he *likes* you? You know, he likes you and he wants you to be the best you can?'

Arnald snorted quietly. 'Does that Prior Benet like you?' he asked scornfully.

Pip tried to imagine a Prior Benet who, in fact, liked him. He couldn't.

'No,' he admitted. 'But Sir Robert's a *completely* different person – trust me!'

There was a pause.

'I guess,' said Arnald, though he didn't sound convinced. 'So, what do we do now?'

'Just have to sit tight till morning,' chirped Perfect. She sounded annoyingly cheerful about the prospect.

'Easy for *you* to say,' Pip growled at her. '*We'll* be frozen lumps by then.'

'Where's my bedwarmer when I need him!' groaned Arnald. His breath showed as lighter puffs of mist in the dark.

'What's a bedwarmer?' asked Pip. He was shivering now too.

'A servant. He heats up big flat stones by the fire, and then he puts them in between the sheets on my bed for a while – warms it up for me.'

'S-sounds wonderful,' said Pip glumly. 'Absolutely wonderful.'

'Huh!' said Perfect. 'Is that all? *I* can do *that!*'

'*What?!*'

'Sure. Pip, you make up a bed with your two cloaks. Go on,' she ordered.

Pip did as he was told, doubling up their cloaks and laying them on the bottom of the punt. With a pleased gurgle, Perfect slipped between the layers.

For a long minute, nothing happened. Then

curiosity made Pip reach a hand towards the lump in the cloaks that was Perfect.

'*Hey!*' he croaked in amazement. 'Hey – it's *warm!*'

Perfect scrabbled about under the cloaks until her head stuck out.

'Come to bed, young sirs – it's a nippy night out there!'

Pip and Arnald did not wait for a second invitation. The floor of the punt might be hard and the space cramped, but with a dragon-shaped hot-water bottle between them, it felt like the height of comfort.

'How do you *do* that?!' asked Arnald.

Perfect giggled smugly. 'Hold my nose and flame a bit,' she said. 'Heat up from the inside out – *and* I can top up the temperature any time I want. Rocks can't do *that!*'

'Goodnight, oh Greater-than-Rocks!'

'Goodnight, King Person.' There was the sound of a gargoyle yawn. 'Goodnight, Pip.'

'Goodnight, Perfect . . .'

Chapter 18

What the Morning Showed

'Give me a boost, will you, Pip?'

It was morning. The boys had slept solidly – and Arnald was showing no sign of wanting to get up anytime soon. Pip was more used to early starts, and had already splashed some icy fen water onto his face as a token wash.

And Perfect had decided it was time for an aerial scouting trip. She clambered up onto Pip's wrist and, balancing carefully, let him fling her, hard into the air. There was a clapping of stone wings, a delighted '*Wheee*' from the gargoyle, and she was aloft.

'But,' Arnald protested from the bottom of the punt, 'that's *crazy*! People will *see* her!'

Pip stood there, his head tipped back, watching Perfect circling, laboriously gaining height.

'They don't, though,' he said. 'People tend to see what they *expect* to see. They'll think she's a harrier, maybe, or some sort of demented duck.'

Arnald didn't look convinced.

Perfect was out of sight now, but Pip didn't sit down. He stood there, thinking, *It's Easter Sunday. I should be singing in the Cathedral right about now.* He waited to feel a huge stab of regret, but it didn't happen.

'What are you *looking* at?!' said Arnald finally.

Pip glanced down, and gave him an odd smile. 'It's a lovely morning, Your Majesty,' he said, making a mocking bow. 'Stand up and see!'

Grumbling and stiff, Arnald did as he was told.

The marshes stretched out to the horizon all around, blurred here and there with banks of mist. The night cold had frost-tipped the reeds and sedge and the clumps of low trees and scrub with silver. Away to the east the sun hung, still low in the sky, making everything spark and glint. The air was fierce and bright and smelled of thin ice and the distant tang of the sea. A skein of geese passed overhead, so low they could see individual feathers and hear the creaking of pinions whenever the general honking let up.

'It's not really *lovely*-' began Arnald. Pip stiffened, preparing to be offended. 'It's more . . . *glorious!*' the King concluded.

They grinned at each other, and were silent for a while. Then . . .

'Pip?'

'Hmm?'

'How *does* she fly?'

Pip shook his head. 'Same way she swims, I guess.'

Arnald looked at him.

'I mean, she's made out of *stone*, right, but she doesn't exactly *swim* like a stone, does she?' said Pip. Then he shrugged. 'Just a mystery. Bit like a miracle.'

'A *lot* like a miracle,' said Arnald.

There was another pause, and then,

'Pip?'

'Yes?'

'I'm sorry I tried to, you know, buy her.'

Pip didn't answer at first. Then he muttered, 'I'm sorry I hit you.'

'That's all right,' said Arnald. 'And I probably won't bother with having you tried for treason. If that's all right with you?'

'Yes. I think I could live with that.'

'Excellent,' said Arnald solemnly. 'So could I.'

Perfect made them both jump by gliding in from behind.

'I'd . . . say that . . . way,' she panted. 'A little . . . south of the sun.'

And Pip agreed. But, as he bent to pick up the pole, Arnald took hold of his sleeve.

'Can I have a go?'

Pip hesitated, looking at the other boy doubtfully. 'It's tricky, you know,' he said. 'And it's hard work.'

Arnald nodded. 'But . . . quite fun, too, though?' he said, pleadingly.

Pip gave in, and grinned. 'Yeah. It is quite fun . . . Come on then. I'll show you how.'

For the next while, their progress was extremely erratic, and marked by a lot of squealing (as freezing water ran up Arnald's sleeves), a number of near-capsizings (where Pip would have to grab Arnald by the belt to stop him, the pole and the boat from parting company) and a good deal of giggling and barging into the reed beds.

They were so absorbed they didn't even hear the bell at first. It wasn't a grand bell, resonant, imposing, inspirational – it sang with the voice of a frog and not the voice of angels. But it was the sweetest bell Pip and Perfect had ever heard, and to them it meant one thing.

'What's that sound?' said Arnald, and Pip and Perfect cried, '*Home!*'

Chapter 19

Sanctuary

Abbot Michael insisted Arnald be housed in the church itself. The laws of sanctuary were clear – no one could harm him or take him away for a month, provided he didn't step outside.

Except for during services, the boys saw very little of each other. Arnald spent most of his waking time with Abbot Michael. Of course it was the Abbot's *duty* to attend his king, but they also seemed to genuinely like each other. It made Pip a bit jealous, he had to admit, but there was a major backlog of chores for him to be catching up on, so he hadn't much free time to fret.

Perfect wasn't a big help. She *said* she was on guard duty in the church – 'I don't think leaving the

King Person's safety in human hands is quite good enough, do you?' – but Pip suspected that *really* she was just worn out by their adventures and was catching up on her sleep on a beam somewhere in out of the weather.

For winter had closed in again almost as soon as they were safely home, and Wickit was cut off from the outside world. Freezing fog hung over the island, bringing visibility down to a few metres, and the reeds and the channels and even the mud of the Fens seized up. Sounds travelled strangely. The bell that called to prayer seemed muffled and unfamiliar, like a ghostbell from a sunken cathedral. Sinister creaking and groaning noises came from the marshes as the freeze tightened its grip. Pip had bad dreams that he couldn't remember, but that nevertheless hung over his days, making him feel uneasy and anxious.

It was as if they were all waiting for something.

In the end, though, Arnald lived in the church for only a few days. Suddenly, there was a thaw, and a dramatic rise in temperature. The sun, having achieved little more than a lighter shade of grey for days, now attacked the mists, thinning and shredding them by the minute. At the morning service, Pip caught Arnald's eye and they exchanged grins.

Then, just after midday, the messenger arrived. Pip was outside the kitchen door cleaning fish, when a punt carrying three strangers came into view. He watched as Brother Paul helped them tie up, and led one of them over to the church where Abbot Michael was standing in the open doorway. The man dropped to one knee, and then the Abbot raised him, and led him inside.

Pip went back to his fish gutting. When he next looked up, the stranger had left the church again and was coming towards him with his two companions from the punt.

'Your abbot has sent us to have some food and drink!' the man said, in a big hearty voice.

'You've come to the right place, then,' Pip grinned up at him. 'Brother Barnard thinks an empty stomach is a sin!'

The man laughed, but before he could go into the kitchen, Pip stopped him.

'Tell me, did Sir Robert send you?' he asked shyly. 'What . . . what has happened at Ely?'

The man waved the others on and hunkered down beside Pip. 'Yes, I'm Sir Robert's man,' he said. 'We headed out as soon as the weather let us.

As for what's happened at Ely, well, the plotters have been arrested. Sir Giles and the Bishop gambled everything, and that's exactly what they lost. But listen – are you the lad? The one that got the King away?'

Pip nodded. 'But how did you know we came here?'

'Well, we were ordered to search everywhere in the marsh,' the messenger said, 'but Sir Robert was pretty certain this was where we'd find the two of you.' He laughed again. 'He said if you frighten a rat, it'll bolt for its hole. So we came here first.'

He stood up and stretched. 'We'll be on our way back to Ely tomorrow, to let Sir Robert know all's well with His Majesty. But the King is to stay here until we can return with a proper retinue. For now, though, let's go and see what your good Brother Barnard has to say to my empty stomach, eh?'

As Pip went down to the shore to dump his pail of fish guts, Brother Paul called to him. He had 'a few things' he needed Pip to do . . .

It was late afternoon before Pip managed to finish off Brother Paul's 'few things.' He'd stacked reeds ready for repairing the outbuilding roofs, tidied the peat pile, scoured the punt inside and out, mucked out the pigsty – he was filthy and his ragged old clothes were a mess and he was totally knackered.

But Brother Barnard wouldn't let him in the kitchen.

'Here, take these,' he said, thrusting a bundle at him. 'Get yourself clean and changed and then go to the Abbot's rooms – you're wanted.'

'Changed?' said Pip, staring stupidly at the bundle in his hands.

'YES, changed, into your new clothes, fool of a boy! The ones they bought you in Ely.' And Brother Barnard waved him away.

Still damp from washing and feeling odd in his new clothes all over again, Pip arrived at Abbot Michael's door and, after a moment's hesitation, knocked.

Chapter 20

God's Eyebrows!

'Come in.'

As Pip entered the room, he saw a stranger sitting with his back to the door, dressed in sumptuous velvet and satin. Abbot Michael looked dowdy and drab in comparison. It was only when the stranger turned to look at him that Pip realised who it was.

'God's Eyebrows!' he exclaimed. 'Arnald?! I didn't recognise you!'

Abbot Michael choked. 'Yes, Pip, this is *your king*,' he said, half-amused, half-appalled.

'Oh . . . sorry,' said Pip and ducked his head awkwardly.

Arnald scrambled to his feet and made a full

formal bow complete with flourishes.

'I owe you my life,' he said. 'How can I repay you?'

Pip grinned shyly, and shrugged.

'I know – I will build Wickit church the highest spire in all my kingdom!' declared Arnald grandly.

'And then order it not to sink into the marsh mud under its own weight?! What a thing it is to be a king . . . ' murmured Abbot Michael in mock awe.

Arnald flushed.

'I like our tower the way it is,' said Pip quietly.

'Then what *can* I do?!' wailed the King. 'Or do you expect me to just forget how you saved my life?!'

Abbot Michael shook his head gently. 'No, my child, I wouldn't want you to forget. A king needs true friends almost more than any other man on earth, and I wouldn't want you to forget any of yours. But you can't give us anything, here at Wickit, because we have enough already. We have everything we need.' His gaze fell as if by chance on Pip and he stroked his chin thoughtfully. 'Though the day may come when your friend might want *more* than our *enough*. Perhaps, when he is older, you could sponsor him to be trained at the Cathedral. He might even rise to Brother Mark's job as Precentor one day . . .'

'I'll do better than that!' said Arnald, the King. 'I'll make him the Bishop. He'll be His Grace Pip, the high and mighty Bishop of Ely . . . and my good friend.' He turned to Pip, suddenly shy. 'What do you say? Shall I make you Bishop of Ely some day? You could live in a palace and tell everybody what to do and make that Prior Benet say prayers for your soul morning, noon and night—'

'Ahem!' said Abbot Michael reprovingly.

Arnald grinned, unrepentant.

'Could we go now, Father? With your permission?' said Pip. 'The King could do with some more practice at punting before he leaves.'

'It's trickier than it looks, Father,' added Arnald.

Abbot Michael waved them away, and the two boys bowed, left the room sedately, closed the door, and then broke into a giggling, shoving run.

Abbot Michael smiled to himself, a secret smile, as he sat in the window of Wickit under God's big sky.

He saw Pip and Arnald emerge and head towards the pier. He'd just started to turn away when, out of the corner of his eye, he thought he saw something drop down towards them from the tower of the church, but he didn't see exactly what. A bat? A bird? A pigeon, maybe?

Must have been.

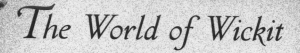

The World of Wickit

(stranger than fiction, weirder than fantasy)

The Keeper of the Wickit Chronicles Answers Your Questions

What big swamp are you talking about here?

The Old Fens were seriously huge, covering thousands of square kilometres and extending into five counties: Cambridgeshire, Norfolk, Suffolk, Lincolnshire and what used to be called Huntingdonshire. They were also seriously dangerous, disease-ridden (malaria, for one), and terrifying . . . Science today would explain those sneaking-up-behind-you noises as 'gas from rotting plants burping to the surface' and those creepy lights as 'spontaneous igniting natural methane'. But lost in the night or the fog, a medieval traveller in the Fens was more likely to remember his sins and fear demons in the dark.

Why are there all those ugly monsters and devils carved on medieval churches?

Perhaps because the stone carvers lived in a time that wasn't all that far removed from pagan beliefs and practices. Some people say that the gargoyles on churches kept evil spirits away, whether by simply scaring them, or by saying, 'This is my patch, shove off,' but nobody really knows anymore. There was a lot of belts-and-braces stuff going on in people's minds in Pip's time.

It made sense to cover all the bases when it came to the dangers of this world, not all of which were physical. (One way to protect yourself from the evil eye is to place your thumb between your index and middle finger while making a fist. You were just as likely to see a monk do this as anybody else.)

Was Perfect ugly?

Of course not. Many gargoyles were ugly or rude, but some of the non-Christian things carved on churches were just as beautiful as she was. Technically, of course, she isn't really a gargoyle at all. You're not a gargoyle unless you're part of the plumbing, with a tube in your throat to help drain rainwater away from the roof. The proper term for Perfect would be a 'Grotesque'. But you'd hardly *want* to call anything as cute as that 'grotesque'.

If Perfect was out there, swimming and flying about, why didn't anybody notice?

Perfect got away with swimming and flying about in the Fenland by being easily mistaken for other things.

Perfect's swimming style would have been to have her front legs (and wings) pulled in along her body, and using a powerful side-to-side tail action for forward propulsion. Half-glimpsed, she probably would have passed for a small otter – the Fens had lots of otters then – or maybe a slightly weird-looking water rat.

In flight she would probably have looked like a pigeon or maybe a rather oddly-shaped hawk. To this day, during courtship, marsh harriers will swoop together, lock claws, and cartwheel in the sky. Any harrier attempting this with Perfect, however, would have been in for a bit of a surprise.

What's a mason's mark? Is it like graffiti?

Travelling stonemasons would sign their work by carving their personal marks on the walls of buildings they'd worked on, sometimes a letter, sometimes a pattern of some sort, like + or ^. The next time you're in a medieval church, have a look for some.

Why is Ely called Ely?

Eels – another creature that the fens were full of. Ely means the 'Island of Eels'. Fen people sometimes used them for paying their rents, and as far as eating went, there wasn't much you *couldn't* do with eels, if you were a medieval cook. They were served stewed, smoked, baked, made into soup, with almond milk or green garlic sauce, jellied or fried or poached . . . though perhaps not as dessert.

What's a posset? For that matter, what's a junket?

A posset was a hot drink of milk curdled with ale or wine with sugar, spices and herbs mixed in. A junket was like liquid cheesecake without the biscuit base.

Why was the place the Prior and Brother John stayed at called the Black Hostelry?

It was called the Black Hostelry because Benedictine monks wore black habits. Having colour coding made it easy to tell them from Cistercian monks whose habits were white, and Franciscan friars who wore grey.

Other than the obvious ones like assassination attempts, were there any downsides to being a medieval king?

The build-up to Easter could be a bit trying. On Maundy Thursday, for example, the King had to personally wash the feet of beggars in whatever town he was visiting. The number of pairs of beggars' feet was supposed to match the number of years old the King was, so Arnald would have got off relatively lightly. Being a king who lived to be 70 or 80, though – well, that doesn't bear thinking about!

I thought they just ate fish during Lent – so what was the Bishop doing offering the King things like goose and beaver for dinner?

Lent was *meant* to be a time when no meat was eaten. How could the Bishop justify serving goose to the King (and presumably himself)? And why are barnacle geese *called* barnacle geese? The answer to both questions is the same. Seeing black and white marked geese at the seaside, and also seeing black and white marked barnacles at the seaside, some bright spark (Gerald of Wales, in fact, in 1188) put the two together, and decided that the barnacle geese *hatched* out of the barnacles. This made them shellfish, obviously, and so eating barnacle geese during Lent was perfectly acceptable. *But beaver?* Well, beavers swim in water; fish swim in water; therefore, beavers are fish. Simple if you know how.

What's a mummer?

It wasn't all fasts and smelly feet in medieval times. There were feast days too. Like Christmas, where you could gorge on things like mincemeat pies (just like ours, but with one addition: real meat!), rabbit in almond milk, pork dumplings in meat sauce . . . anything tasty that wasn't fish! And at Christmas, in the towns, you might get to go and see the mummers, who acted out stories like 'St. George and the Seven

Champions of Christendom' at Christmas time. It was a bit like school plays today that you get dragged to because your little sister's bagged the role of the Third Shepherd on the Right. Except that mummers were all grown men, and you were expected to pay them.

I'm not sure I actually want to know, but what is night-soil?

Night-soil was whatever a household put into their chamber pots overnight. Flush toilets were still a long way into the future.

Why did monks have a bald patch?

A tonsure was the shaved patch on the top of monks' heads, leaving a circle of hair round it, like the crown of thorns Jesus wore on the cross. The monks didn't shave them every day – there were set times of year for sprucing up your ton sure – so there must have been a fair amount of itchy stubble to scratch in between.

Where did Brother Gilbert's medicines come from?

Cooking and medicine weren't so far apart in Pip's day. The Infirmarer and the Cellarer often used the same ingredients. Take Brother Gilbert's cold cures, for example. You could make a poultice – a sticky hot mess of flour and water and things like mustard – in the kitchen and then put it on your patient's chest to help draw out illness.

St. John's Wort (for arthritis), vervain (for fever), greater celandine (for vomiting and warts) and shepherd's purse (to stop bleeding) are British plants he would have used, but some of the ingredients in medieval medicines came from as far afield as India and China. Imported cinnamon bark was used to treat diarrhoea. Myrrh was used on wounds. Saffron from Turkey was used to treat infections as well as in cooking.

When Abbot Michael was ill, Brother Gilbert made medicine for him made up of a number of different things, based on the advice of different authorities. He chose lungwort, for example, on the basis of the Doctrine of Signatures. Lungwort is a plant with spotted leaves that look like diseased lungs. Some medieval sages thought that God made it look like that so that humans would know it was good for treating chesty conditions. Brother Gilbert chose thyme because it is a herb traditionally used in folk remedies. And he chose liquorice because it was recommended as far back as the ancient Greek, Hippocrates, for coughs and colds. The end result had a little bit of everything in it – more belts-and-braces!

Another local plant was belladonna (also known as 'deadly nightshade' and 'dwale'). Though it is certainly poisonous, very small quantities of it were used in medieval medicine to treat many things, from sore throats to typhoid.

And then there was ginger . . . ginger was thought to be a remedy for the plague (otherwise known as the Black Death). It was *also* suspected of provoking the sin of lust – but was widely used in cooking and medicine anyway!

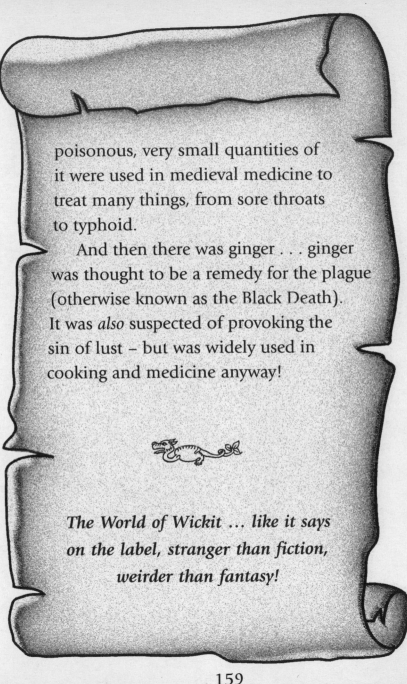

The World of Wickit ... like it says on the label, stranger than fiction, weirder than fantasy!